“Stay, Danie

“All right. I’m s

some of the darkest parts of my past hidden from ye. I don’t want your head soiled with such horrible memories.”

“And I’ve hidden things from you,” she confessed.

“Ben?”

A gentle, rosy blush painted across her cheeks. “Yes. I loved him, Daniel. I–I. . .”

“Of course ye loved him. That doesn’t bother me.”

“Really?”

“Of course not. You married him for love. I could never take that place in your heart.”

“That’s the problem, Daniel, you are.”

“What are ye sayin’?” He laid down beside her and cradled her in his arms.

“I’ve fallen in love with you, Daniel Greene. I know you didn’t marry me for love, and I don’t expect you to love me the way I love you. . .”

LYNN A. COLEMAN, raised on Martha's Vineyard, now calls Miami, Florida, home. She is a multi-published award-winning author and the co-founder and president of the American Christian Romance Writers, an international writing organization. She is a minister's wife who writes to the Lord's glory. She has three grown children and seven grandchildren. She also hosts an online workshop for writers of inspirational fiction. Lynn invites you to visit her website: www.lynncoleman.com.

HEARTSONG PRESENTS

Books by Lynn A. Coleman
HP314—Sea Escape
HP396—A Time to Embrace
HP425—Mustering Courage

Lizzy's Hope

Lynn A. Coleman

Heartsong Presents

I'd like to dedicate this book to my son, Timothy Daniel Coleman, God's promise to me fulfilled. May the Lord continue to bless you and your wife as you continue to build your relationship together.

A note from the author:
I love to hear from my readers! You may correspond with me by writing:

Lynn A. Coleman
Author Relations
PO Box 719
Uhrichsville, OH 44683

ISBN 1-58660-376-0

LIZZY'S HOPE

All Scripture quotations, unless otherwise noted, are taken from the King James Version of the Bible.

Cover design by Robyn Martins.

PRINTED IN THE U.S.A.

one

Key West, 1866

"Evenin'. Miz. Lizzy?"

A massive chest caught Lizzy's gaze as she opened the door. Slowly, she raised her head. A large, dark man with mahogany eyes and squared shoulders towered over her. She tightened her grasp around the glass doorknob.

"Yes, may I help you?"

His shoulders eased. His rigid stance softened. "Mr. Ellis sent me here."

In turn, she loosened her grip of the knob.

"Come in," she offered with a smile.

Ellis Southard, a local businessman, had become more than her mother's employer. He and his new wife, Bea, had become some of her closest friends.

"Thank ye, Ma'am." He lifted his straw hat from the top of his head and stooped to enter through the doorway.

"Take a seat, Mr. . . ?" She hesitated, realizing she'd forgotten to ask the man his name.

"Name's Mo."

The large rattan chair creaked as his huge body mass eased down. It wasn't that he was a heavy man. Lizzy doubted there was an ounce of fat on him. His broad shoulders were well rounded with thick muscles. His hands were massive, and yet also agile, she noticed, as he curled the edges of his Bahamian hat.

"So, what does Mr. Ellis have need of?" She sat on the sofa opposite Mo's chair.

"No, Ma'am, Mr. Ellis don't need nothin'. I's afraid I misled ye."

Her eyes caught the glimmer where his wrists marred with encircling dark scars. Lizzy scanned the house to catch sight of someone, anyone, she could call if necessary. She had lived with her brother George and his family since her husband Ben had gone off to fight in the war. When Ben had died, her stay with her brother and his family had become permanent.

"Mr. Ellis sed ye might be able to help me. It be embarassin' to ask, bein' a grown man and all." The hat in his hands twisted into unnatural shapes. "Mr. Ellis, he figures ye understand. And bein' that yer helpin' the young'uns, ye be understandin' why I, uh, need this help." His shoulders slumped. His eyes looked down at his feet.

"Relax, Mo." She'd seen folks like this far too often. If her suspicions were correct, he didn't know how to read or write. "If Mr. Ellis sent you here, I guess he figures I might be able to help you."

He stopped fumbling with his hat, leaned forward, and lowered his voice. "I cain't read or write."

"And Mr. Ellis thought I might be able to teach you?"

"Yes'm. He be showin' me some letters and makin' me practice 'em, but he ain't got no times for me." He pulled out a crumpled piece of paper and handed it to her. A series of As and Bs lined the page. "At least not 'nuff so's I can learn faster. I wanna learn."

She examined the letters more closely. He had a steady hand, but the deep impressions on the paper showed he worked with intensity.

"I can pay ye. I know ye teach the young'uns, and I's a working man. I can come after work or on the Lord's day. Don't seem right to have schoolin' on the Lord's day—but ifin it's all the time ye can give me, I be a willin'."

She could give him a couple evenings a week, and the extra income would help. She loved her brother George and his family, but she desperately needed a place of her own. Of course, a widow with four children finding earning enough for the family would be quite an undertaking, but it was her secret dream and hope.

"Which evenings would you be free, Mo?"

"Whatever be best fer ye." Mo settled into the high back of the rattan chair, resting his hat on his left knee.

Lizzy clicked her right first fingernail on the arm of the sofa. She usually went to church with her mother and the children on Wednesdays, and on Fridays her mother often came by. "My best nights would be Tuesdays and Thursdays. How about around seven?"

"Seven's fine, Ma'am. Would I be needin' to buy anything?"

"Some paper, a pen, and some ink would be helpful."

Mo nodded his head. "I can git them, Ma'am."

"Momma." A whine broke through the hushed atmosphere. "Benjamin's picking on me." Sarah came running into the room.

"Excuse me, Mo." Lizzy removed herself from the sofa and pulled her daughter by the hand toward the back door. "Benjamin Joseph Hunte, what have you been doing to your sister?"

Her slender son shrugged his shoulders. "Nothing."

"Whatever 'nothing' is, you'd better behave. I have company in the front room, and I don't need you children making a fuss." Lizzy leaned over to Sarah. "Now, you go play, and don't you start picking on Benjamin either."

"Yes, Ma'am." Sarah's braided pigtails bobbed with her nod of agreement.

"Good. Now go play." Lizzy tapped her daughter's backside as she jumped down the stairs.

Lizzy walked through the kitchen and back to the front room. "I'm sorry about that."

"No trouble. I best git goin'. Shall I come tomorrow night, it bein' Tuesday and all?"

"Sure, Mo, tomorrow will be fine."

He rose from the chair and again Lizzy was struck by his size. "Thank ye kindly, Ma'am. I do appreciate ye takin' on the likes of me."

"Don't think of it. I've taught a few adults how to read and write. There's no shame in it."

Mo nodded and bent his head to exit the door. For a man so tall, he certainly seemed gentle. Lizzy couldn't help but notice the scars on his wrists. . .former slave, she imagined. Her jaw tightened and her fists curled, nails biting into her palms. She took in a deep breath, counted to three, and eased it out slowly. She had lost her husband in the war against such things. Ben's parents had been slaves too, but they had won their freedom in the Bahamas. Lizzy's parents never were slaves, so she hadn't known the pain, fear, and anger firsthand. But she'd seen enough over the years, and the very idea of someone owning another human being made her skin crawl. When would she be free of this anger? She didn't hate like she used to, but she still burned with fury when she saw someone like Mo, scarred and illiterate because some slave owner thought the color of one's skin determined his or her intelligence.

"Jesus, thank You for letting me grow up here. Help me deal better with the pain of the injustice." She mumbled her prayer and returned to the kitchen. "Dinnertime is coming, and ten people with hungry bellies will be wanting to be fed. So you better get your mind to your work, Lizzy," she chided herself as she went to the sink to clean her hands.

❧

Mo placed the hat back on his head and ambled out of Lizzy Hunte's front yard. Palm trees lined the road heading inland toward his own place. A smile spread from ear to ear. "I be a learnin' man in no time at all. Thank Ye, Lord."

Mo looked back at the house, now distant. "She be a fine woman, that Lizzy Hunte." Her home was a simple but serviceable structure, he noticed, with a coral foundation, clapboard siding, and a pitched roof. Why anyone would need a pitched roof in Key West didn't make sense to him. Pitched roofs were for snow and ice-bound houses. Word was, the first owners of the island came from the north.

Mo thought back on his previous visit with Ellis Southard in his home where he'd met Lizzy Hunte's mother, Cook.

She be a fireball, he thought, remembering how she had stood her ground. And yet Lizzy seemed not to have that same self-assurance her mother possessed. *Course, losin' a husband and havin' four young'uns to raise probably factored in on that.*

Lizzy had taken a quick glance at his wrists. Not much a man could do to hide 'em, especially down in this heat. Mo slowed his step and wiped his brow. The sun beat down on the pulverized coral streets, and a fine white dust filled the air around him. He glanced to the west and could see the sun lowering on the horizon. So different than the cotton fields back in Alabama. The blue, flat surface of the water turned to crimson red, then caught the streaks of the last rays of the setting sun before it slipped quietly below the horizon.

Yup, this place sure was different than the plantation. His mind flashed back to the sweet smile on Lizzy's face when he'd mentioned Ellis Southard. His name relaxed her. *She feared me, though,* Mo realized with a sigh. Seemed most folks he met feared him. Sometimes being built like an ox didn't come in handy.

Of course, he was used to it. Folks just had a problem with someone as tall as himself. He'd yet to meet a doorway he could go through without bending. A knot tightened in his stomach. That wasn't exactly correct. The southern mansion his master had owned had a door he could have walked through. Two his size could have walked through it shoulder to shoulder.

His mind darkened. The past, the beatings—all of it swirled in confusion and anger. He'd escaped eight years ago and still the memories haunted him.

"Evenin', Mo." James Earl waved from his porch.

"Evenin', James."

"Been out walkin'?"

"Some." James was a kindly old man. His graying hair and eyebrows accented the wrinkles that lined his face.

"Wouldn't be courtin' now, would ya?"

Mo chuckled. "No, Sa. I's not ready to find me a woman."

He wanted to know how to read and write first. He knew he'd have to sign a marriage license if he were ever to marry, and without being able to read the license, he didn't trust anyone. He could be signing on as someone's servant and never have a clue until they came to get him for work. *No siree, I'm not signin' no papers until I knows how to read and write.*

"Seems to me you're old enough, and you've got a good job." James tapped his pipe on his porch railing.

"Thirty years ain't that old."

James rapped his hand on his knee and let out a guffaw. "Son, you've been old enough for a decade."

Mo thought back. "I fell in love once."

"What happened?"

Mo sat on the step of James's house, removed his hat, and worked the brim with his hands. "My master decided to bed her, just to show me who wuz in charge."

James got up and settled beside Mo on the steps. "I'm sorry, Son. I earned my freedom when I was a young man. How'd you earn yours?"

"Escaped! After my master took Caron, she didn't want no part of me. I was just so mad that I up and run to freedom. When the war came, I signed up. They promised freedom for every Negro man who fought fer the Union Army fer a year and wages after that. So I fought."

James placed a hand on Mo's shoulder.

"I never did see Caron again or the plantation. I heard the South ransacked the house and took most of the food, but I never saw it to knows ifin it be true or not."

"How long were you on the run?"

"Three years. Kinda hard to hide, being as tall as I am. But I worked my way west for a spell, then went north. I had a mean master. Some folks didn't have it quite so bad. But I did. Truth be told, I think my master wuz afraid of me, so he set out to try and scare me every chance he git. I stood head and shoulders over the man."

James chuckled. "You're a big one. How tall are ya?"

"The Army said six foot, nine inches. But them trousers they gave me were still a couple inches too short. So I guess I be closer to seven feet."

James let out a slow whistle. "And how big was your master?"

Mo's chest rumbled with laughter. "Tiny little man, maybe five foot seven."

"No wonder he was afraid of you. You could have crushed him with one hand."

"Oh no, I couldn't do that. As bad as the man wuz, I couldn't of killed him. Ain't right to take a man's life, no matter how bad that man is to ye. Not to say I didn't think it a time or two, but no, God wouldn't be pleased. War's different. But I never git used to seein' a man fall because of my own hands. I took more prisoners than a lot of men. Most were so full of anger they didn't mind killin' off every Reb they came in contact with. Just ain't right."

"You're a wise man, Mo. Not too many understand and accept God's forgiveness."

"I wouldn't say I's all that wise, just tryin' to live by the Good Book."

❧

"Was that Mo Greene I saw leaving here, Lizzy?" George asked as he came into the kitchen and washed his hands.

"Yes."

George dried his hands. "Is love in the air?"

"Goodness, no, George. He's needing someone to teach him how to read and write. And don't you be spreading that around either."

"My lips are sealed. He's a good man, Lizzy."

"How do you know him? He seemed nice."

"Met him at Ellis's dock a time or two." George leaned over the simmering pot. "Dinner smells great; what are we having tonight?"

"Chicken and dumplings, just like the ones Mom used to make." Lizzy grinned.

"Now, Sis, you're a fine cook and all, but no one can make them like Mom," George teased.

"Perhaps you better tell me that after you've eaten. I think I figured out her secret ingredient." In fact, she'd finally gotten her mother to tell her the truth for the entire recipe. The secret ingredient was a spice in the biscuits, or rather, the right combination of spices. Lizzy grinned.

"Did I miss something?" George lifted the pot lid.

"Momma, Ben's pickin' on me again," Sarah whined.

"Did not."

"Were too." Sarah stomped her foot.

"Nah-uh, you were foolish enough to go fetch it," Benjamin defended.

Lizzy looked at Sarah's legs full of muck and mud, and some scratches from briars, no doubt. "Sarah, get yourself outside and cleaned up right now."

Lizzy placed her hands on her hips, then turned toward her son and watched his grin instantly dissolve. "And you, Benjamin Joseph, what do you have to say for yourself?"

"Aww, Ma, it's her fault. She kept daring me."

"And you, being the older, don't have enough sense not to let your sister's teasing get the best of you?" She tapped her foot for emphasis.

"I'm sorry." He bent his head low and looked at his bare toes.

"How's a mother supposed to make a living knowing she can't leave her young'uns at home without them getting into trouble?"

"I'm sorry."

"I've got work tomorrow cleaning for Mr. Sanchez. How am I to go and not concern myself with you misbehaving?"

"It won't happen again, Mom."

"You're right it won't, and you'll be painting the chicken coop tomorrow for your Uncle George just to remind you not to get all caught up with your sister's teasing."

"But, Ma, that ain't fair."

"Isn't, not ain't."

"But it isn't fair, Ma. Sarah ought to have to do something too."

"I'm the parent, I'll decide who gets what punishment. And you're right, life isn't fair. Never has been, never will be."

Benjamin held his tongue. She could see his little mind working. As for Sarah, she'd have to think up a real good punishment for her. Not only was she teasing Benjamin but tattling as well, exonerating herself in the process, or so she thought.

George's wife, Clarissa, walked in with her three children. "Smells great, Lizzy." Clarissa gazed back and forth between Benjamin and Lizzy, then over to George, who nodded.

"Thank you, Clarissa. Dinner's done cooking when everyone's ready to come to the table." Lizzy went to lift the large pot from the stove.

George called the household to the table. The family of three adults and seven children sat down to pray. Lizzy examined each of their faces. So many people under such a small roof. Perhaps tutoring Mo was the answer to her prayers?

two

Lizzy snuggled under the covers and rolled to her side. She had another fifteen minutes of rest before she had to get up, and she was bound and determined to get it. Division of the household duties worked well: Clarissa made breakfast and lunches, Lizzy cooked the dinners. That allowed her the opportunity to teach the children while preparing dinner. She punched her feather pillow and snuggled in deeper.

Olivia's little hands and feet cuddled up next to her. She never knew her father. In fact, she wasn't sure Benjamin had even known he had a second daughter when he died. Lizzy took comfort in knowing Ben could look down from heaven and see their little true blessing. She rolled over and caressed Olivia's cherub cheeks. "Morning."

"Morning, Momma."

"Did you sleep well?"

"Yes, Ma'am. Can I go to work with you?"

Lizzy lifted her head off the pillow. "No, Darling, you know I can't take you to work with me."

"I know." Olivia's large oval eyes looked into her own. "Momma, why do you have to work?"

Rip my heart out, Child. Out of all her children, she thought Olivia at least would be used to her working. "Honey, you know I have to."

"I know, it's just that I don't want you to. Sarah says that before Daddy went off to war you stayed home and took care of her and Ben."

Ah, Sarah again. Perhaps the punishment for teasing Ben yesterday might not have been tough enough. "True, but I still worked, Dear. I used to do some people's mending to earn a few extra dollars."

"Momma, why'd God invent dollars?"

Lizzy chuckled. "Actually, God didn't invent money, man did."

"Well if God didn't, why do we have to have 'em?"

"Them not ' 'em,' " she corrected.

"Them?"

"Liv, I don't know if there is an easy answer to that one. I do know that it's the easiest way to get what you need. For example, we don't live on a farm and don't have enough room to have a herd of cattle so we can have the hides to make shoes. So with money I can buy the shoes from someone who makes them, and he can buy more leather to make more shoes."

"But wouldn't it be better if we didn't need money and everyone just gave everyone what they needed?"

"Now, Girl, that's heaven, and we don't live there yet." Lizzy sat up in the bed.

Olivia's white cotton chemise accented her creamy chestnut skin and her bright hazel eyes sparkled. "Daddy's in heaven, right, Momma?"

"Right, Sweetheart."

"Then Daddy doesn't need money, right, Momma?"

"Right." Lizzy slipped on a cotton robe she kept on the bedpost and cinched it at the waist.

"But we still do, right, Momma?"

"Right." How Lizzy wished she could stay at home with her children. God saw fit to take Benjamin, though, and somehow He was going to be providing for her and the children. She just hadn't figured out exactly how yet. Her mother helped with bills, since she earned a good living and had few expenses. But Lizzy wasn't fond of charity; family made it easier. From as far back as she could remember this house had been always filled with someone from someplace—generally the Bahamas, where her parents came from. Her mother had moved out seven or eight months ago and moved into Ellis Southard's house. That gave the house a little break, allowing the older children to share their grandmother's room.

In all fairness, it wasn't hard living with George and Clarissa, and Lizzy always felt useful. She couldn't charge the parents who allowed their children to be schooled; it didn't seem right. Few of the families had any real extra. Of course they often would share some extra fish, lobster, or fruits and vegetables they harvested. Thank the good Lord there was never a lack on their table.

She was also thankful she could teach the children and didn't have to keep it a secret, the way folks had to on the plantations before the war. Of course, black children weren't allowed to go to the island academy. On the other hand, lots of families taught their children in their homes. Some said the children concentrated better at home. Others said it was better to have professional learning. In either event, Lizzy was the teacher for any of the island children who came by. Often it was difficult because the children were not consistent. But the need for an education, the need to learn to read and write, was growing like rapid fire among her people. And that was another sign of the changes that had started since the end of the war.

"Momma?"

Olivia's sweet voice brought her out of her reverie. "Yes?"

"Will I ever go to work with you?"

"Not likely, but I might be able to let you visit Grandma one day while I'm working."

"So I can play with Richie?" Olivia's curls bounced up and down. She always enjoyed playing with Bea's nephew.

"Of course. Now go get dressed."

"Thank you, Momma."

"You're welcome, Sweetheart." Now if only her mother was as excited about the prospect as Olivia. Lizzy chuckled. Her mother loved children but ruled them with an iron hand. Although in recent days Lizzy had noticed that her mother was letting the grandchildren get away with more, and she was definitely feeding them more cookies.

Lizzy shook off the image of her mother and joined the family in the kitchen. Her nose caught the scent of the bacon before her ears heard it sizzling on the griddle.

❧

Mo scanned the horizon. The ocean had a slight chop, but not enough to prevent the men from gathering their sponges today. Mr. Southard had told Mo that if he learned to read and write he'd be able to promote him to foreman over the divers. He'd always wanted to learn to read and write, but the job promotion reignited the old dream. And for the first time in his life he believed it could be possible. On the plantation he hadn't been allowed. Now. . .well, now things were different. Mo grinned and aligned his face with the sun. "Thank Ye, Lord," he said for the millionth time since Lizzy Hunte had agreed to teach him.

"Good morning, Mo, how are you?" Ellis Southard walked up behind him on the dock.

"Fine, Sa. Feelin' mighty fine."

"Did you speak with Lizzy?" Ellis grinned and surveyed the dock with a watchful eye.

"That I did, Sa, and she be agreein' to teach me."

"Wonderful. I figured she would."

"Mr. Ellis, would it be a problem if while I'm sponging ifin I could be pickin' up some conchs to sell? I wanna pay Miz. Lizzy fer the lessons, and the extra will come in handy if I goin' to be learnin' a couple days a week."

"Sure, just as long as you keep your quota of sponges up, I don't have a problem with it." Ellis bent down to pick up one of the long hooked poles they used to gather the sponges.

"I checked 'em all before ye came." Mo pointed to the far end of the line of equipment. "That one I's thinkin' we need to replace. Depends on whether or not the man has a light hand, I suppose."

"If you think it's weak, I'll purchase another. Let's see if we can brace it in the meantime."

Long poles were not something you could harvest from the

island. Ellis would need to order them. *And that's why I be needin' to read and write. A foreman cain't order ifin he cain't read an invoice.*

Ellis sat down on his haunches and examined the pole, then grabbed it with both hands and bent it over his knee. "Good call, Mo. The grain's ready to snap."

Mo nodded his head. He liked Ellis Southard; he was the kind of human being one could appreciate. Rumor had it he once stood up to a man who insulted one of his black guests. Mo hadn't been on the island when that happened, but from what he knew of Ellis Southard, he could see him doing it.

Ellis interrupted his thoughts. "Can you get me a couple of shunts and some sturdy twine?"

"Yes, Sa." Mo ambled into the small building at the end of the dock. Inside was an assortment of sponging equipment and a small desk where Ellis worked on his paperwork. Mo found himself looking at the papers and even recognized his name, Mo, in a couple of places. There were numbers but he couldn't make any sense out of what they meant. He only knew that Ellis Southard paid him well and paid him fairly from week to week. Most weeks it was the same pay, but once in a while he'd get more if he worked an extra day, and occasionally he'd get less if the day was too bad and they couldn't go out. On the other hand, Ellis was good about allowing a man to go out for a second haul, if the time and weather permitted it, to make up for the lost day. "Yes Sa, he be a right good boss. Thank Ye, Lord."

Mo picked up a couple small strips of wood and a ball of twine. "Here ye go, Mr. Southard."

"Thanks." Ellis worked the shunts around the weakened area of the pole and fastened them to it with the twine. He wrapped the twine tightly and evenly around the area.

"Fine job."

Ellis nodded.

The other men started to arrive for their day of work. Most were reliable but once in a while you got one or two who wouldn't make it because they spent the night drinking. Each man took his small skiff, loaded up his poles, knives, and nets, and set out. Mo was always the last to leave, making sure everyone had what he needed.

"Mo, I'd like to have you stay at the dock today. You'll get the same pay but I need some help washing and drying the sponges."

"Yes, Sa. Whatever ye need."

Mo worked long and hard in the hot sun. One thing about diving for the sponges was that being in the water cooled him down some. Unfortunately, the water in the south was nothing like he'd experienced in the north. He'd taken baths cooler than that ocean some days. Even during the winter, he'd learned that the waters didn't chill much. Often they were warmer than the air.

❧

By lunch the entire dock was covered with sponges drying in the hot, tropical sun. "Mr. Ellis, what do ye wanna do with those sponges still in the vat?"

"They'll have to continue to soak for another day or so—no other place to set them out to dry."

"What about the roof of the shed? We could put up a net around the edge so as they won't be blowin' away. Seems a shame to let that space go to waste," Mo suggested.

Ellis scratched his beard. "Good idea, Mo."

As the divers came in with their day's haul, Ellis and Mo were putting on the finishing touches of the net wall around the perimeter of the shed's roof. Mo continued working on the roof while Ellis helped the men put the new sponges in the soaking vats. Mo covered half the roof with the sponges in need of drying. Tomorrow the other half could be set up. Stretching his back, Mo worked the kinks out and proceeded down the ladder.

"Mr. Ellis, may I take a skiff out?"

"Day's done, Mo. What do you need it for?"

Mo shuffled his feet. "I want to try and git a few conchs to sell."

"I'm sorry. I forgot you mentioned that earlier." Ellis reached into his pocket and pulled out a couple silver dollars. "Here, take this as a bonus for your suggestion for drying the sponges on the roof."

"No need, Sa."

Ellis reached for his hand and placed the coins into Mo's palm. "Mo, take it with my appreciation."

"Thank ye, Sa. I don't knows what to say."

"Thank you is just fine. Learn lots tonight. I'm looking forward to training you to be my foreman."

Mo nodded his head and headed down the dock toward his home. A small room in a boardinghouse served his needs, though there were times when he'd wished for a bit more elbow room.

Mo turned a corner off of Front Street. A sharp pain to the back of his head sent a flash of bright light across his vision before everything went pitch black.

❧

The children cleaned up the kitchen and dishes from the evening meal as a part of their chores while Lizzy went through her limited supply of materials under her bed. She pulled out some basic charts for writing letters. Tonight she'd concentrate on the letter C and have Mo hear several words that began with A, B, and C. *That should keep the man busy enough for one night,* she hoped. Especially when she taught him that C had two sounds, not just one. Lizzy pictured him trying to keep C straight once they hit K and S.

"Momma, can George Jr. and I go outside to play?" Benjamin hollered from somewhere behind her.

"Sure, for a little while."

"Thanks, Ma."

"Momma," Sarah called.

"Yes, Sarah."

"Can I go outside and play too?"

Lizzy got to her feet after replacing the supplies under the bed. "Yes." If she was going to have a moment's peace she needed reinforcements from George and Clarissa.

"George, Clarissa?" She wandered to the back bedroom, their private sanctuary.

George popped his head out the door. "What do you need, Sis?"

"Mo's coming for his first lesson today and it appears that the children need lots of attention."

George held up his hand. "Say no more. Come on, Honey, let's take the young'uns outside for a spell."

"Wonderful idea, George," Clarissa called from behind him. "Don't worry none, Lizzy. We'll keep 'em out of your hair."

"Thanks. He's real nervous."

"We understand."

Lizzy looked at the clock. *Fifteen minutes, great.* She put a bucket of water on the stove so everyone could wash up with warm water when they returned from outside. In the dining area she set out the alphabet cards, a slate, and some chalk. She also placed a dog-eared homemade book on the table. She'd drawn and painted items for each letter, and each letter had its own page. For years she'd used it, and it continued to be one of her best teaching aids for the children.

She glanced at the clock again. Seven o'clock. He hadn't seemed like the kind of man who would be late. Then again, everyone on Key West went by a different kind of clock, called island time. Some said it came from the Spanish, some said it just came from the heat. Everything slowed down a pace or two, especially during the height of the day.

Lizzy went to the back door and watched George wrestle the older children. Perhaps she should have put on two buckets of water, she mused. Clarissa had the younger ones engaged in a story. She caught another glimpse of the clock. Maybe he forgot? Or maybe he just decided he was too embarrassed to show his ignorance when it came to book learning? She'd wait a few more minutes.

George had two boys holding onto his legs as he attempted to walk across the yard. George grunted. The boys laughed and sat on top of his feet.

"Mr. Mo not coming?" Vanessa, her niece, whispered from a chair in the kitchen.

"He should be here shortly. Something could have delayed him. What are you doing in the corner?"

"Reading. I didn't want to go outside and get dirty again." Vanessa scrunched up her nose and placed her hands on the book she was reading.

"What are you reading?"

"Little Briar Rose."

The front door rattled in its hinges. "Coming!" Lizzy called.

"Must be Mr. Mo," Vanessa offered and lowered her gaze back to the book in her lap.

"I imagine so. Enjoy your stories." Lizzy rushed to the front door and pulled it open. A scream tore from her throat. "Help!"

three

"Help me, please." Mo's hoarse whisper sent chills down Lizzy's spine. She leapt out and grabbed him. A crimson red trail covered the back of his head and neck.

"What?" George came running up huffing and puffing. "Let me help you." George sidled up and placed Mo's left arm across his shoulders.

"Let's bring him over there to sit down." Hearing Clarissa and the children gasp, Lizzy handed out orders. "Clarissa, get me a sharp needle and thread. Vanessa, some clean rags. Ben, get some of the hot water from the stove."

George and Lizzy sat Mo on the chair. "What happened?" they asked in unison.

"I wuz headin' home from work and someone hit me from behind."

"Hard," George added.

Lizzy worked her fingers around the wound, examining it.

"I don't recall much of anythin' else, 'cept comin' to. I knew y'all be spectin' me so's I came here. Sorry."

"Don't be apologizing. Let's see how much damage they did." Lizzy carefully blotted the area with a cloth Vanessa brought. His short nappy hair was scarlet. "There's a cut about an inch long, not too deep. I'll need to clean it out."

"I appreciate ye helping. A man cain't do much fer himself workin' behind his eyes." Mo's head nodded forward.

Is he going to lose consciousness again? "George Jr., would you bring a glass of water for Mr. Mo?"

"Yes, Ma'am." Lizzy heard his footsteps heading into the kitchen.

"Thank you." Lizzy looked at her brother. "Did you see anyone?"

"No, Ma'am."

She saw the inside of Mo's pockets were hanging out. "Have any money on you?"

Mo fumbled for his pant pockets. "Appears to be missin'."

George interrupted, "Was it a lot?"

"Had a couple silver dollars."

"I'll get the sheriff," George offered.

"Don't think it will help. Feller hit me before I saw anythin'."

"Perhaps so, but the officials need to know this has happened." George headed for the door.

"Someone must have seen Mr. Ellis payin' me," Mo mumbled.

Lizzy placed her hand on his shoulder. "Shh, relax. Let George fetch the sheriff."

Clarissa returned with the needle and thread, and soon the children brought her the various items she'd requested. Everyone huddled around Mo and stared.

Olivia's gaze widened. "Is he going to die, Momma?"

Goodness, the children didn't need to see this, and they certainly didn't need to see her stitching up the man. "No, Darling. There's only a small cut on his head. Head wounds just bleed a lot." Granted there was more blood than normal, and he probably had a concussion too, but if he could make it here, she was sure he would be fine.

Lizzy fixed her attention on Clarissa. Soon their eyes met, and Lizzy motioned for her to corral the children and bring them to the other room.

"Come on, children. I think your Aunt Lizzy has everything under control. Why don't we go clean up and get ready for bed?"

Lizzy cleaned the blood off the back of Mo's neck and shoulders, sopping up as much as possible from his hair. "Are you okay, Mo? Any dizziness?"

"I's a bit unsteady on my feet but I be all right."

"I need to stitch up that wound."

"Let me show ye a trick I learned in the army. Helps with the stitchin'. I'll need a lit candle and the needle."

She placed a dry rag against the wound and encouraged him to hold it there. "I'll be right back." Lizzy wondered what a candle could be used for, but he seemed to know what he wanted. Being in the Army, she reckoned, more than one man needed some stitching from time to time.

She returned and lit the candle, placing it on the small tea table in front of the sofa. He picked up the needle and heated it until it was red hot. He used the wooden spool and pushed the needle's head down on it in a rolling manner. The needle now had a slight hook shape to it.

"With head wounds the bone of the skull is close to the surface. So's this here needle will cut into the skin but will start coming back sooner. Just hook the other side of the torn skin and it will come out."

Lizzy nodded. It seemed to make sense, but she'd never worked with a hooked needle before. "I'll do my best. This will hurt."

"I trust ye."

Mo's hands clasped the arms of the chair after she threaded the needle. "Don't fret, Mo. I need to shave off some of your hair around the wound first. Don't want hair in the wound."

Mo nodded and released his grip on the chair.

❧

He heard Lizzy coming before he could see her. In her hand she held a straight-edge razor. "I'll be careful."

Mo grinned. "I's not worried about ye. Ye have a gentle touch, unlike some."

Lizzy knitted her eyebrows but refrained from asking her obvious question. He respected that. She had no idea about the scars on his back or the events that led up to getting them. Thank the good Lord she was raised in a place like this, where she was never owned, never treated like. . . Mo shook his head. No, Sa, he wasn't going to think about those things again.

"I'm sorry, did I hurt you?"

"Huh?" Mo hadn't felt a thing. What did she mean?

"You shook your head just as I was about to shave near the wound."

"Sorry, I's wasn't payin' attention. I keep it still fer now on."

"First lesson, Mo. Don't say I's, simply say I. You'll find I'm a stickler for proper grammar."

"I don't understand whatcha talkin' 'bout, but I will do as ye say. At least try."

Lizzy's smile lit up the room; her bright white teeth were like a fine string of pearls on a wonderful sea of amber gold. But even her smile couldn't dull the pain. His head throbbed. Whoever had whacked him hit him real good. The sun was setting when he'd come to, so he must have been out awhile.

"Mo, I'm going to start stitching now."

Lizzy's words snapped him back to the present. "Go ahead." Mo braced for the pain, knowing it couldn't be much worse.

"This works great." Lizzy tugged away at his flesh. Her gentle fingers contradicted the pain. A mixture of warmth from a woman's loving touch and a desire to scream caused him to curl his lips and hold them shut.

"Two more, Mo, and I'll be through."

He lifted a hand and waved off the comment, certain if he spoke he would have been less than a man, and moaned.

"I'm tying the last one, Mo."

He released his hold of the chair, then worked his fingers to bring the blood back into them.

"Momma, Aunt Clarissa said to give Mr. Mo this." Sarah brought in a tall glass of limeade.

Mo reached out for the glass. "Thank ye, Miss."

"Tell Aunt Clarissa Mo's all stitched up."

"Okay, Momma. Are you feeling better, Mr. Mo?" Sarah whispered.

"Some. I think a night of rest will fix me up real good."

Sarah nodded and walked into the kitchen.

"Let me look at your eyes, Mo." Lizzy waited for him to turn and look at her.

"I's, I mean, I am fine, Miss Lizzy—just feel like a mule kicked me in the head."

Lizzy chuckled, then sobered. "At least a mule you know how to watch out for. Do you think whoever did this was after your money?"

"Don't know. Coulda been I suppose, hard to say. Coulda been they's were hard up fer a drink."

"Maybe. Still seems odd for a man to knock out the likes of you." Lizzy flushed. "I mean with you being as tall as you are and all."

Mo grinned and gently tapped the top of her hand. "I know what ye mean. Probably why they hit me from behind."

George came running through the door. "Sheriff is on his way."

Sweat poured down the back of George's neck and stained the collar and armpits of his shirt. "You should not have run," Lizzy commented.

"A man needs his exercise, especially after wrestling the youngsters in the backyard. Didn't know I was that out of shape. Getting old I suppose." George sat down on the sofa.

Clarissa came in with a glass of water. "The children are ready for bed but I told them they could read or practice their schooling for a bit before they go to sleep." She sat down beside her husband and handed him the water, then leaned toward everyone and whispered, "I'm willing to bet they're all by the door trying to listen in."

Lizzy smiled. "I wouldn't put it past them. Once the sheriff comes and goes we'll let them out."

"After the sheriff comes, I better git to my place," Mo said. "No sense in tryin' to learn with this here headache."

The screen door rattled in its hinges as a loud knock hit the door.

"Come in," Lizzy, George, and Clarissa called out.

"Mr. Ellis!" Their voices sounded in unison as they jumped up from their seats.

"Sit down. Mo, what happened?" Ellis came up beside him.

"Someone hit me."

"Took his money too," George added.

"Did you see anyone?"

"No, Sa. They's come at me from behind."

"How bad's the injury?" Ellis asked and sat on the stool by the rattan chair.

Lizzy spoke. "Cut's about an inch long, took five stitches. I could see the skull. They hit him pretty hard."

Ellis nodded.

The door banged again, but this time it opened immediately.

"Mr. Ellis, ya walk like there's a fire." Cook placed her hands on her ample hips.

"I'm sorry, Cook. I didn't know you were coming too."

"Course not, ya ran out of that house like the good Lord Himself had hit ya with a bolt of lightning." Cook chuckled and hugged her daughter.

"Hi, Mom." Lizzy was a taller, thinner version of her mother. They shared the same almond shaped eyes, although Lizzy's were hazel and Cook's brown. It was obvious to Mo where Lizzy got her beauty.

"Now who be foolhardy enough to mess with the likes of you, Mr. Greene?" Cook addressed him. He had to grin; she was a take-charge kind of woman. He'd met her on more than one occasion, and he honestly liked the woman.

"Appears they weren't just fools, since they's hit me from behind."

"Chickens."

"Grandma!" The seven children couldn't contain themselves any longer and ran into the front room. Mo knew he was the reason for all this bustle in the house tonight. He imagined something was always keeping this house hopping like a brown lizard in search of a warm rock.

The door rattled again. Mo got up and met a man he

assumed was the sheriff. "Mo?" the man asked.

"Yes, Sa. Let's take this outside and I tell ye what happened." The sheriff stepped back into the front yard and Mo followed. He turned back when he heard the door open. Mr. Ellis and George came out to join them.

"Tell me what happened." The sheriff's voice was firm.

❧

"All right, children, that's enough excitement for one day. Let's get to bed and don't forget to say your prayers." Lizzy shooed the children off to bed. She busied herself with helping the younger ones brush their teeth and hair. Being naturally curious, she wanted to be out front and hear what the sheriff would do, if anything.

Course he always has been fair to the Negroes on the island, she reminded herself. *Why is it still so difficult to trust a white man after all this time?* Perhaps she'd never openly trust anyone, but she was willing to work on it and allow folks the benefit of the doubt. Her friendship with Bea Southard had helped tremendously in that regard. But sometimes she wished she could be more like Bea, less assuming of the bad and more accepting of the good, until the person proved themselves unworthy.

She returned to the front room to see her mother listening at the doorway. Lizzy chuckled. "Hear anything, Mom?"

Francine jumped. "I didn't hear ya come in."

"No, that's quite obvious."

"Oh, don't ya go fussing with me, you wanna know just as much as I do."

"True, but it doesn't make it right, and I'm not the one hovering at the door."

"Humph." Her mother came and joined her on the sofa. "So, you're going to teach Mo?"

"Yes, I'm hoping the extra income will be enough for me to get a place of my own for myself and the children."

Lizzy felt her muscles relax as her mother placed a warm wrinkled hand on her knee. "Getting crowded?"

Lizzy chuckled. "Getting? You made your escape."

"True, but I didn't bring any young'uns with me." Francine smiled.

"Be happy to share some," Lizzy teased.

Clarissa walked in and added, "Me too."

Francine roared with laughter. "No, thank ya. I've raised mine, now it's your turn to raise yours. I'll just spoil 'em rotten for ya."

"Thanks, Mom," Lizzy responded.

"How much money did they get?" Clarissa steered the conversation back to what was on all of their hearts.

"He said a couple silver dollars."

"Mr. Ellis mentioned something to Bea about him givin' Mo a couple silver pieces earlier in the day," Francine put in. "Something about him earning a bonus."

Ellis Southard was a kind man, but Lizzy hadn't heard of him being free with money. He'd always seemed mighty conservative in that regard, so if he gave Mo that kind of a bonus, whatever Mo had done for Mr. Ellis must have been worth the pay.

"Can I get you something to drink, Mom?" Lizzy offered.

"No, thank you, I'm fine."

"How's Bea doing?"

"She's been sick in the mornings, but she feels better around the middle of the day."

"When's the baby due?" Clarissa asked.

"She's figuring he'll come around Christmas," Francine offered. "You should see Mr. Ellis parading around the house proud as can be."

Lizzy chuckled. "I remember Ben when he first learned I was in the motherly way. Never saw that man smile more."

Clarissa grinned. "George was the same way."

"Ahh," Francine said. "But my George, he's got ya'll beat. When he found out I was a carryin' his young'uns he ran to the paper to place an announcement. The editor congratulated him but let him know as gently as possible that ya don't place a birth announcement before the baby is born. When George stood up in church the next Sunday, I was about ready to crawl under the pew. I was so scared he'd tell everyone."

"What's so funny?" George asked, coming inside.

"We're just talking about your father, Dear." Francine got up from her seat. "Guess it's time I headed home. Good night all."

Ellis paused. "Mo, would you like me to walk you home?"

"No, Sa, I be fine." Mo hesitated at the door. "Thank ye fer speakin' on my behalf with the sheriff."

"I figured it wouldn't hurt to add my character reference for you. Not that it was necessary. Sheriff already seemed to know who you were."

"Appears so." Mo slumped his shoulders.

"You're a big man, Mo Greene, and dark. Some folks just get nervous," Lizzy suggested.

"I knows, but I'm glad the sheriff, he knows I always kept to myself." Mo's legs wobbled and he grabbed the doorknob for support.

"Mo, sit down before you go banging up the front side of your skull," Lizzy demanded.

Ellis helped him to the sofa. "Maybe I should call the doctor."

"No, I's fine, Mr. Ellis. I been hit harder. Just need to rest 'tis all."

"You can spend the night on the sofa," Lizzy offered.

"I's, I mean, I don't wanna impose on ye none."

"It's no imposition, right, George, Clarissa?"

"Nope, none at all."

Ellis headed back to the door. "I'm going to take Cook home, then I'll stop over to Mo's place and pick him up some clean clothes." Ellis left before Mo could respond.

George cleared his throat. "It's late. I've got to go to work early, so I'll say good night, unless you need something, Lizzy."

"I'm fine. I can handle getting Mr. Greene settled. You two

get some sleep. It's been a mighty full day."

"Night, Mo. I'll say a prayer for you." Clarissa joined hands with her husband and walked down the hall to their room.

"Did you eat, Mo?"

" 'Fraid not. Could. . ." He paused. "I trouble ye for some hot tea?"

"No trouble at all. I'll even bring you some leftover lobster and shrimp casserole I made."

"Thank ye, I'm too hungry to play humble and turn ye down tonight." Mo grinned. He was a large but gentle man. Lizzy headed into the kitchen and placed the kettle on the stove to heat up some water for tea. She watched his hands, how he'd played his fingers along the edge of his hat a few days ago, how he caressed his fingers over a book when he thought she wasn't looking. She wondered how it would feel to have his fingers caress her cheek with the same wonder and adoration. . . *Oh my, what brought that crazy thought into my head?* Lizzy fanned herself, waving off her wayward thoughts.

"Lizzy?" Mo whispered.

four

Mo walked up beside Lizzy and placed his hand on her shoulder. She jumped.

"I didn't mean to scare ye. I's sorry."

"Sorry, I was daydreaming. You just startled me." Lizzy wiped her hands on a towel.

"I wuz looking fer. . .the. . ." Mo tucked his hands in his pockets, looked down, and shuffled his feet.

"Ahh, it's in the backyard, to the left."

"Thank ye."

She placed a bowl, a loaf of bread, some jam, and a spoon on the table. Before Mo came back from the outhouse, Ellis Southard had brought a bundle of his clothes. When Lizzy returned to the kitchen and didn't find Mo, she opened the back door to see if he was in trouble. She certainly hoped not. She always figured herself to be a strong woman, but helping the man to a chair earlier this evening showed her just how weak she was. The door on the outhouse creaked open and she eased out a pent up breath. *Thank You, Lord,* she silently prayed.

"Come in and sit down. Your dinner is all fixed for you."

"Thank ye, Miss. Lizzy, I don't know how to be repayin' ye fer all your kindness."

"Nonsense, it's nothing any good Christian wouldn't have done." Lizzy sat across from him at the small oak table.

"All the same, ye don't know me, not really, and you've opened yer home to me. I appreciate it." Mo grinned and bowed his head for a silent prayer.

"If I'm not being nosy, how badly does the loss of the silver dollars affect you?"

"A week's worth of lessons, I'm afraid." Mo forked up a large chunk of lobster. "This is mighty fine vittles. Thank ye."

"Vittles?"

"Food. Sorry, an expression I picked up from some fellers headin' west."

"Just how much of this country have you seen?" Lizzy loved the thought of traveling. So many ships from so many countries passed through Key West harbor. They gave her wanderlust.

"A fair amount. I wuz running fer a long time. Didn't wanna stay too long in one place. As ye notice I's. . .I," he corrected himself, "ain't exactly able to blend into a crowd."

"I suppose that would be true. You escaped?"

"Yes'm. I could take the beatin's, I just couldn't take. . ." Mo let his words trail off.

"Sorry, I didn't mean to upset you. I've seen slavery, but not as severe as I've heard stories about. I'm one of the fortunate few who was never owned by anyone."

"When you're young it's easier. Once you're older and understand not every man is owned. . .well, gits a bit hard to live with. One of the hardest things about accepting Christ as my Lord was the verses the preacher would say about being a slave for Christ. And if you're a slave, to stay put and show your faith. I failed the good Lord on that one. But I know he ain't holdin' it against me." Mo pushed his plate away from him and patted his stomach. "Thank ye. That be a fine meal."

"You're welcome." Lizzy found herself warming to the man's compliment. "I better get some linens for you to sleep on. I've set a pot on the stove for you to wash with. There's soap and a rag by the sink, and this towel hanging over the chair is for you to dry yourself."

"Thank ye."

Lizzy made a hasty retreat. Caring for a man would crumble the wall she'd built around her heart. *You're just reacting to the injustice,* she decided, attempting to fortify herself. Although she had to admit his dark molasses eyes drew her attention, like the sunlight kissing the ocean. She fought to keep herself firmly planted on solid ground.

❧

Mo woke early, his head still pounding. Restless, he got up and folded the linens and placed them on the sofa. He tiptoed out of the house, praying he wouldn't wake anyone. Dawn lingered on the eastern horizon as he headed for the waterfront and Ellis Southard's wharf. If he caught the tide just right he'd be able to catch some snappers for breakfast, a small payment for the kindness of Lizzy's family.

Pulling in half a dozen fish, he set his poles back in the small cubby that Ellis provided him. Roosters still crowed in the distance as he ambled back up the streets toward Lizzy's home. Mo squinted, shielding his eyes from the direct assault of the bright morning sun's rays. Soon he found himself back at Lizzy's home, gently knocking on the front door.

Lizzy opened the door and smiled. "Mo. I was wondering where you wandered off to."

"Done me some fishin'. Thought youse folks might like some fresh fish fer breakfast."

"Thank you, Mo, but that wasn't necessary."

"Seems little enough to say 'thank ye,' but I'd appreciate your takin' these."

Lizzy reached out and took the string of fish.

Mo tipped his hat. "I best be goin' now. I need to git myself to work."

Lizzy's soft satin touch on his arm sent a ripple of warmth through his body. He'd be needing to guard himself against such foolish desires. After all, Lizzy was educated; he was not.

She saw him glance down at her hand on his dark arm, her amber skin's creamy perfection against his scarred body. Yes, he could not let his wayward thoughts travel far. Everything inside him shouted how wrong he was for her, how there could be no future in any thoughts or desires of a romantic nature. He looked into her eyes, eyes that sparkled green and gray this morning. He loved her eyes, always changing, never the same.

"Mo, don't dive today. An infection might settle in the

wound. You can't mess with head wounds. They're just too close to the brain."

"I's a-hopin' Mr. Ellis. . ."

"I hope," she corrected.

"I hope Mr. Ellis will have some dock work for me, or I might not be able to start my classes fer another week."

"I'll pray for you, Mo," Lizzy offered.

Mo blinked at the gentle words. No one had ever offered to pray for him since he left his mother and escaped from the plantation. He suspected his mother was still praying for him, and it warmed him during some of his darkest moments.

"Would you like to stay for breakfast?"

"No, thank ye. Old James Earl, he likes having me come fer morning breakfast. I suspect he likes the company."

"I understand. Have a good day, Mo. I'll see you when you're ready to resume your lessons."

Mo tipped his hat and exited the small but comfortable home. For a house of ten people it didn't seem overcrowded. There was love in that home, and for the first time in many years he truly missed his home on the plantation. He missed his mother, his brothers and sisters. What were their lives like now?

❧

Lizzy's next few mornings at work were busy. Mr. Sanchez was away on business in Cuba, and Mrs. Sanchez had her scrubbing every closet and airing every room for a good spring cleaning. Lizzy could understand why Mrs. Sanchez waited for Mr. Sanchez to go out of town.

Mo hadn't come by for two days since his accident. The stolen money must have really put a hole in his pocket, she surmised.

Of course today was Friday and payday. Perhaps he would feel free to come and learn tonight, she hoped. For some reason she wanted to help Mo, wanted him to be able to read and write. To be able to get a higher position working for Mr. Ellis could only be a good thing, she reasoned.

"Momma?"

"Yes, Olivia."

"Is Mr. Mo coming to learn tonight?"

"I don't know, Sweetheart. I hope so."

Olivia played with a folded piece of paper in her hands.

"What do you have there?"

"Something."

"And 'something' is?"

"A present." She turned her chin down to her chest and drew a circle on the floor with her big toe.

"And can I ask who the present is for?" Lizzy continued.

"Mr. Mo."

"Oh." She hadn't talked much with the children about Mo or his accident, but obviously it left an impression on her delicate little water lily. Of all her children, Olivia had the lightest skin and the same sharp nose and features as herself.

William came running in through the front door all huffing and puffing. "William, what's the matter?" Lizzy asked.

"I won," William gasped.

"You won what?"

"A race with Mr. Mo."

Mo was running? Didn't the man know he'd cause blood to rush to that head wound? "Where did you meet Mr. Mo?"

"Down by the salt farms."

"And what on earth were you doing down there?" Lizzy placed her hands on her hips.

"I was looking for work."

"Work! William, what on earth are you talking about? A five-year-old boy doesn't go looking for work."

"But Ben said if we all got a job we could get our own house."

"Benjamin!" Lizzy hollered. *If that boy doesn't stop trying to be the man of the house, I'm going to. . .okay maybe I wouldn't go that far. But goodness, Lord, do something about that child.*

Mo rapped on the door. "Come in, Mo. I'll be right with

you," Lizzy answered, then turned to shout, "Benjamin Joseph Hunte, where are you?"

"Here, Momma. What's the matter?"

"Did you tell William to get a job?"

"Wellll." Benjamin pushed his hands down into his pants pockets. "Sort of."

"What do you mean by 'sort of'? And if you're all fired up about earning money, why aren't you out looking for a job?"

Benjamin looked shocked.

"Exactly. If you're going to be asking your brother and sisters to go to work, you've got to be willing to do it as well. And since you're the oldest, I'll be expecting you to work twice as many hours and bring home twice as much pay."

"But, Ma," Ben whined.

"Well?"

"But what about playing?"

"Oh, a man can't be playing. He has to work. And since you're all fired up about working, I guess you want to be the man. And if you're going to be the man, you best be getting a good job and working the kind of hours your Uncle George puts in every day, leaving the house first thing in the morning and not getting home until supper time."

His wide brown eyes widened even further as he gulped down her words.

"I expect you to have a job by the time we finish supper. Go on, shoo! Go find a job so you can pay for all of us to have our own home, and I won't have to work for Mr. Sanchez and can just stay here and take care of the house and the other children's learning. Go on now." Lizzy waved her hands toward the door.

Slowly he walked to the front door.

"Go on, you've got ten minutes. Better hurry."

"Ten minutes, Mom? I can't get a job in ten minutes."

"You can't get a job anywhere. You're too young. And your foolish words had your five-year-old brother down by the salt farms. Now go to your room and think about what you did and what it is to be an adult. We'll discuss the matter later."

"Yes, Ma'am." Benjamin quickened his pace and headed into his room.

❧

Mo thought how wonderfully wise Lizzy was. On the other hand, he also envied the boy's life. He'd started working on the plantation by the time he was four. Play was done quietly and away from the master's view.

"Hi," Mo offered, when she came in the room wagging her head from side to side.

"I swear that boy comes up with more brilliant ideas than God has stars in the night sky."

"He's creative."

Lizzy chuckled. "Thanks for bringing William home. I didn't even know he was gone."

"Just happened to be in the right place at the right time, I suppose." Mo reached into his pocket and pulled out a nickel. "Apparently he'd worked fer a while before I found him. The owner of the farm wanted him to have this. Says he gathered a couple pounds of salt. He also sed when he's older to send him to the farm and he'll hire him on the spot."

Lizzy chuckled and took the five-cent piece from Mo. "Thanks. I'm sure he'll enjoy buying some candy with this."

"Would ye be able to teach me this evening after yer dinner?"

"Of course. How's your head?"

"No more headaches, thank the good Lord. But I needs to rise slowly or it causes some pain."

"Did Mr. Ellis have work for you?"

"Some, but I fished fer the sponges from the boat, just didn't dive in after any."

Lizzy nodded.

Mo tucked his hat back on his head. "I'll see ye later then."

"All right, and thanks again." Lizzy followed him to the door. "Would you like to have dinner with us?"

"I's wouldn't wanna be any trouble."

"No imposition. I'm making conch chowder and fritters."

"Mmm. You're sure I won't be a bother?"

Lizzy reached out and touched his arm. "Mo, it's the least I can do after you rescued William."

For some strange reason he'd hoped she would say she enjoyed his company—of course, she hadn't really experienced his company before this. He'd only come briefly to ask her to teach him, and then he arrived battered and in need of some help. The memory of her hands touching him, like now. . . so soft and light. . .satiny. . . Mo cleared his throat. "Anyone would have helped."

"Perhaps, but not anyone did, and God obviously put you in the right place at the right time for a reason. Now, I know you mustn't get a home-cooked meal all that often, so let me treat you."

Mo grinned. "Home-cooked would be mighty nice, thank ye, Miss Lizzy."

"You're welcome. You can make yourself at home in the living room, or you can return in forty-five minutes." Lizzy headed into the kitchen.

"Ifin ye don't mind, I'd like to return. I's got some errands."

"Okay, see you later."

Mo waved good-bye and headed for home. He needed to bathe. Salt water and sweat didn't make a man smell fresh. *Now why am I's so concerned about how I smell?* he mused.

five

Later that evening, with the house quiet, Lizzy sat beside Mo at the table. Hunched over, he practiced penning the letter C. "That looks great, Mo. Now here is the hard part about the letter C. It has two sounds. One sound is like another letter, the letter K. For example, words like cap, cake, cookie—all start with the letter C but have the harder sound."

Mo nodded.

"The other sound of the letter C is like the letter S, but often that is when C is in the middle of the word, not the beginning."

"Ifin youse says so. I's don't know what those other letters even look like."

Lizzy penned a copy of the letters K and S for Mo, pointing to which was which. "Now think of the hard sound for the letter C. What words have your heard that use that sound?"

"Cake. . .cookie. . ." he repeated. "Conch?"

"Good! Conch does begin with the letter C." And on and on they went, discussing various words that began with C. Then Lizzy moved on to the letter D.

As they discussed the sound of D and the various other letters, he asked, "Does Daniel begin with D?"

"Yes, Daniel begins with D. And the second letter is A, which you've already learned."

Mo's face lit up.

"Why do you ask, Mo?"

" 'Cause that be my name. My real name. Everyone calls me Mo, so I go by it. But the name me mother called me wuz Daniel."

"How'd you ever get a nickname like Mo if your name is Daniel?" Lizzy asked.

" 'Tis my own fault, I suppose. When I's. . .I mean, I signed up to fight I wuz asked to make my mark. And not wantin' to appear like I didn't know how to write,. I put two letters that I seen together and figured they would sound like Mo."

Lizzy giggled. "You'll have to tell me more. How'd you know the letter M?"

"From signs on stores. And I knew the stores were markets or mercantiles. So I figured it be an M sound. The O come from No Trespassin' signs. And I figured if thar could be a small word like no, why couldn't thar be a small word like Mo?"

"Well, you figured correctly, Daniel. Would it be all right if I call you Daniel?"

"I be honored, Miss Lizzy. I's not been called Daniel fer five years. Sounds mighty fine coming from ye."

Lizzy fought down a slight blush. "Would you like to see your full name written out?"

"Yes'm."

"This will be your homework, practicing your first name."

"All right."

Lizzy watched as Mo, correction, Daniel, saw his name unfold before him. Like a child caught in the wonder of a bee gathering honey from a flower, Daniel savored every pen stroke. Then she handed him the pen. "Here, you try once."

The only trouble he had was with the letter E, which she had noticed many folks seemed to find troublesome when beginning to write.

"Excellent, Daniel," she praised.

"I thank ye kindly, Miss Lizzy. I can almost feel it in my bones. I'm goin' to learn to read. I be educated."

Lizzy grinned. "Yes, you will. But remember, you already have a lot of learning in you. This is just one area that you've never been allowed to develop."

"I best be goin'. I need to git up early tomorrow."

"Good night, Daniel."

"Good night, Miss Lizzy. I see ye tomorrow, ifin that's all right."

"Tomorrow's fine." She hadn't been planning on teaching him tomorrow, but it would work out just fine.

"Who's Daniel?" George called from the den.

❧

Mo couldn't believe his good fortune. In the past few weeks he'd learned all the letters of the alphabet, his numbers, and how to write his own name. He was beginning to read some of the earlier readers, but he wasn't as confident in reading out loud as he was in writing on paper. Mr. Ellis was genuinely pleased with his progress and began to explain the various ledgers and books he kept. Mr. Ellis's books weren't as easy as Miss Lizzy's. . *.but them be the kind I really need to learn,* he reminded himself.

"Course, Miss Lizzy's purdier to look at." Mo grinned as he said the words out loud. "On the other hand, she has four children." Mo felt his grin slip. What was a man to do? How was he supposed to court a woman with a ready-made family? And would she even be interested in having a man around? On the other hand, she did seem to smile when he walked in the room. *Course, she's probably just thinkin' how fast I'm learnin'.*

Mo kicked a chunk of coral on the path between his home and James Earl's. The elderly gentleman had been pleased to hear that Mo was learning to read and write. James hadn't learned much, but he knew some.

"Morning, James," Mo called as he opened the screen door.

No response.

Mo paused and listened.

Then he went to the back of the cottage and looked out in the yard. Not seeing his friend, he called again, "James?"

No response. Mo headed to the back door and called again.

Still no answer. Mo's heart hammered in his chest. He turned the knob and entered the kitchen. The scent of death crossed his nostrils. "No, Lord," Mo moaned and ran to James's bedroom.

The old man's still body lay sprawled on the bed, semi-covered by a clean white sheet. His skin was ashen. Mo stepped forward and cradled the cold, lifeless hand of his friend. A salty tear burned a blazing trail down his cheek. James Earl was gone. A man who had become like a father to him.

Mo never knew his own father. He'd died the winter Mo turned two. James's wife had passed on many years ago, and they had never been blessed with children. So Mo always figured he and James were good for each other.

Friendship demanded that Mo do his duty to see James buried next to his wife. He set to washing and dressing his old friend, then got the undertaker. He'd planned a morning lesson with Lizzy, but now he penned a quick, clumsy note and paid a boy a nickel to deliver it. His words were simple: "No Come, Daniel." He figured he could explain later, but he hoped it would be enough for her to understand.

"Rev, I needs your help," Mo told the pastor while gulping in some air.

"What can I do for you, Mo?"

"James Earl is dead. I found him this mornin' in his bed. I cleaned and dressed him, and the undertaker is coming by. But I need ye to come to the house and see if he left any important papers."

"I reckon I could do that." The preacher set his wide brimmed white hat on his head and followed Mo.

"How'd you know James Earl, Mo?"

"I been seein' him every mornin' since I first came to Key West. He is a kind old man and needed some company."

"True, James hasn't been able to get about much any more. I'm glad he had a friend in you."

In truth, Mo was the man who was blessed to have a friend like James, but he wasn't so sure the pastor would understand if he shared his thoughts.

At James Earl's they found the undertaker arriving with his horse-drawn hearse. Mo fought the images of the past, of watching folks carrying the dead to a small section of the master's land. The women wailing. . .the men somber during their funeral march. . .battlefield images of men being buried with no one to mourn.

Mo left the pastor to speak with the undertaker and went into James Earl's home one more time. What should he do with James's personal effects? Who would you send them to when there wasn't any family? James had to have a brother or sister, some kind of family somewhere. They'd want to know. They'd need to know. Mo searched through a small desk in the front sitting room. A few old letters and a note with "Daniel" written on it, but Mo couldn't figure out the writing on the inside. He hadn't learned to read this style of lettering yet. Mo tucked the letter in his pocket. Mr. Ellis or Lizzy could read it for him.

"Mo," the preacher called as he walked in.

"In here, Pastor. Just goin' through his desk, seein' ifin I can find some letters from family."

The pastor picked up a folded paper with fancy lettering on top. "This is his will, Mo."

Mo's hand stopped digging through the drawers. "That'll be telling us who to notify, right, Pastor?"

"Yes, it should." The pastor unfastened the fresh white papers that crinkled when opened. "I, James Earl," he read, "being of sound mind, do hereby give all my worldly possessions to Mr. Daniel Greene of Key West, Florida." The pastor paused. "I don't know a Daniel Greene. Is he a relative of yours, Mo?"

Mo wanted to stick his finger in his ear to clear it. He couldn't believe what he just heard. James gave him all his earthly possessions? Why? The pastor's dark eyes darted back and forth catching Mo's attention. "Sorry, what did ye say?"

"I was wondering if you know this Daniel Greene."

"That would be me, Sa."

"Pardon me?"

"My name is Daniel, Daniel Greene. I've been goin' by

Mo fer many years, but my given name is Daniel."

"Well then, it appears that James has left you all his worldly possessions."

"I knows not what to say. I knows not what I will do with James's possessions. I only have a small room."

The pastor scanned the document further, then chuckled. "Mo, I'm not sure how to tell you this—but James owns this house and the land it sits on. This paper says you now own it."

"James owns this house? I cain't believe it. James wuz a poor man, just like me. He didn't have nothing fancy, nothing. . .he owns the house?" Mo collapsed in the maple chair.

"He did. Now it's yours."

"He never told me. Ye certain?"

❧

Lizzy smiled at the young boy with a missing front tooth. "Can I help you?"

"Mr. Mo said to give ya this." He thrust a piece of crumpled paper toward her.

"Thank you."

"Bye." The boy waved and jumped off the steps, landing with both feet on the ground in a squatting position. He jumped up and ran off.

Places to go and things to do, she mused. Lizzy opened the crumpled note. The message was simple, and she certainly understood its meaning. She smiled at how well Daniel had constructed his letters. She glanced at the note again. What could be keeping him away this morning? After they'd begun lessons a few weeks ago, he'd never missed a session.

Perhaps Mr. Ellis had some additional work for him, she decided. With her morning plans changed, she had a few free hours to herself. George and Clarissa had taken the children for a morning fishing trip.

Lizzy felt so out of place in her family's home. *A few hours to myself and I can't enjoy it. I need my own home.* "Lord, I still feel like I'm intruding on George and Clarissa. It was easier when Momma lived here, seemed more like her home then." Today, she just didn't feel a part of the place.

"I'll go visit Momma and Bea. Haven't seen them in ages," she told the Lord, and headed out the door.

As she walked down the street and headed toward Front Street, a horse-drawn hearse passed. Lizzy crushed her hands to her sides. A part of her could never accept that her husband was buried in some unmarked grave. And yet that was reality. Death with no grave to mourn at left her feeling incomplete. Graves certainly served a purpose. She didn't see herself going to her husband's grave on a regular basis. But once in awhile, when she was feeling blue, it might have been a place where her soul could sit and reflect on the love they had, on the lives they had brought into the world, and somehow rejoice that God was in control.

Lizzy entered the Southards' property but faltered as she was heading for the front door. Mr. Ellis had bought this place nearly a year ago, and he had hired her mother to work full-time for him. Mr. Sanchez required Lizzy to enter through the servant's door in the rear. She raised her hand and knocked on the solid oak door.

"Lizzy. Come in, come in." Bea smiled. "It's so good to see you."

Lizzy stepped into her friend's open arms and hugged her. "How are you feeling?"

"Better. I'm still getting sick in the mornings, but just a little."

"I remember with Benjamin I was up night and day. . . Can't believe I actually wanted another child after I went through the first."

Bea laughed. "Let me get through this one before we talk about another."

"Lizzy?" Her mother came out of the kitchen, wiping her hands on a dishtowel.

"Hi, Mom. How are you?"

"Fine, is everything all right?"

"Nothing is wrong. Mo couldn't come this morning for his

lesson, and the children have gone off with George and Clarissa. I thought I'd share a cup of tea with you two, if it's all right?"

"Of course." Francine headed back to the kitchen. "I'll go put on the kettle."

"Come, sit in the parlor with me." Bea led her to the front sitting room, and sat on the sofa beside her. "So, tell me about teaching Mo."

"He's a fast learner."

"Ellis said he's grasping things very quickly," Bea added.

"He is. I don't think I've ever had an adult more interested. So how's Richie?"

"He's fine. He and Ellis went for a sail. I was invited, but the very idea of riding up and down on those waves. . ." Bea placed a hand on her stomach.

Lizzy laughed. "No need to explain."

Francine came into the parlor with a tray of fresh biscuits and a silver bowl with guava jelly. "A morning for girl talk." Francine beamed. "I love it."

Lizzy smiled. She loved it too. It had been ages since she was free from the children, work, or other responsibilities. The ladies chatted for a while, and finally Lizzy shared her heart. "I just feel I need my own place."

Bea patted the top of Lizzy's hand. "I think I understand."

"Makes sense, but how ya going to afford it?" Francine asked.

"I make a fair pay cleaning for the Sanchezes, and I've been saving. But I honestly don't know how I'm going to manage it. Ben was a good man, but he didn't own any property, and he certainly didn't know how to save for the future. Not that he had all that much time to save."

"I could probably help you with some money to buy a place," Bea offered.

"Oh no, I couldn't do that. It wouldn't be right. And I figure if I can't afford to rent a home what makes me think I can afford to keep one up?"

"Well, the offer still stands if something comes up."

"Thank you, it's a very generous offer." Lizzy still had to fight the lines in her mind between white and black—what white folks did or didn't do. Her friendship with Bea had been slowly dissolving those images. Granted, there were many a folk out there that fit her previous image. But she was beginning to see that not everything was black and white—literally.

"What ya need is a man." Francine placed her china teacup in the saucer.

"I don't think I'll ever be ready for another man."

"Nonsense. You're young, healthy, and attractive. Any man would be proud to have you as a wife."

"I'm also the mother of four children. Not any man could take on that kind of responsibility. Not to mention, I'm not sure I'd want to be married and birthing more babies."

Bea chuckled. "I'm beginning to understand that."

Francine's chest bounced up and down with laughter. "You might have a point there. But a good man. . ."

"Mother, please. I'm really not ready to think of another man. Just this morning, on my way here, a hearse passed. I, I, well I just felt the grief all over again. I loved Ben. I miss him." Salty tears burned at the edges of her eyes.

six

Mo held the legal document in his hands. It just didn't seem right for him to be owning James Earl's property. On the other hand, it didn't seem right to turn down a man's final request. What was he to do? He didn't need a house. A small room suited him just fine. *A house? What's a man like me to do with a house?* Mo tossed his head from side to side.

He needed to put this will in a safe place. But where should he put it? Some folks might not believe he had inherited the property.

The pastor had left after making arrangements for the funeral service that evening. He also promised to spread the word. Mo figured he should probably be telling folks about James, but who should he tell? Who knew him? James hadn't talked about many folks here on the island. He talked some about his wife, but mostly he had listened to Mo talk about his life, his job, and his past. James's sympathetic ear had brought some healing to Mo's memories of the plantation and the beast who had called himself his master.

Mo got up and began to pace. The house had small doorways, he noted, as he bent down to enter from one room to the next. "Ifin I am goin' to be living here, Lord, I need to fix them doors."

Mo stepped out the back door and looked around the yard, taking a mental inventory of what was there and what wasn't. He latched the back door from inside and exited by the front.

"Mr. Ellis can help me. He has one of them fancy safes for his house. Lord, I's not sure why Youse decided to take James at this time, and I's not sure why he gave me his home, but I ask Ye to help me be worthy of such a gift."

Mo knocked on the front door of Ellis Southard's home.

"Mornin', Cook. Is Mr. Ellis here?"

"I'm afraid not, Mo. What's the matter?"

"I's needin' a favor. I can come back."

Cook grasped his arm as he turned. "Mo, Miss Bea is here. Can she help ya?"

"What can I do for you, Mo?" Bea asked, entering the front hall.

"I need a safe place to keep this." He handed her the will.

"What on earth? Mo, why do you have this man's will?" Bea asked.

"James Earl passed last night. I visit him every mornin' and well, I found him. The pastor, he found this here will and, well, he said I needed to put it in a safe place. I knows Mr. Ellis has that fancy wall safe and thought he might be able to keep it for me for a spell."

"I'm sure he wouldn't mind. I'm sorry to hear about your friend." Bea reached out and placed a gentle hand on his forearm.

"Thank ye, Mrs. Southard. I appreciate that."

Mo's eyes caught the slight figure of someone else in the hallway. His gaze set on Lizzy's lovely face. "Miss Lizzy," he said softly and smiled.

"Daniel, did I hear correctly that James Earl died last night?" Lizzy asked, stepping closer to him. Her movements were as graceful as a dove's.

Mo shook off his wayward thoughts. "I's. . ."

"I'm," she corrected.

Mo's jaw tightened. "I'm afraid so."

"I'm sorry to hear that. I know you spent a fair amount of time with him. Was he sick?"

"No, that's the surprise of it. He wuz talkin' last night about all his grand plans for the future." Mo looked down at his sandled feet. "It wuz a shock."

❧

"Come on in and sit a spell. Tell us what needs doin' and we'll be happy to lend a hand. Won't we, Lizzy?" Her mother ushered Daniel toward the front room.

"Of course."

"I already arranged the funeral service tonight, and he be buried tomorrow after the morning service. Too hot to wait until Monday."

Francine nodded her head.

Bea offered to put James Earl's will on her husband's desk until he got home and could put it in the safe. They talked about the meal they should fix for folks and decided to meet in James Earl's home. Lizzy offered to go to James's home and check out his pots and pans so they'd know what they needed. Soon she and Mo were headed out the door.

"Thank ye for the help, Miss Lizzy. I don't knows what I do without youse and Cook's help."

"You're welcome and we're glad to help. Another correction in your speaking. . ." Lizzy paused; she didn't want to overstep her teaching role in Mo's life. "The word is know, not knows. A nose is what you have on your face, and they're spelled differently."

Mo gave a stilted nod.

Lizzy reached out and touched his huge forearm. It was solid, proving his strength equaled his size. Daniel stopped and placed his hand over hers.

"I didn't mean to correct you at Mr. Ellis's, Daniel. I'm sorry about that."

"I appreciate the help, but in front of others ain't helpful, it's, it's. . ."

"Insulting. I know. I'm very sorry. My mother and Bea are the two closest people I have in my life. I don't think of them as public. But they aren't your family."

"No, they ain't, and, yes, it bothered me."

"Daniel, I am sorry. I promise not to do it again."

He caressed the top of her hand with his thumb. Her lighter skin against his darker complexion sent a bolt of awareness that he was a man and she was a woman, singeing her fingertips. Lizzy lifted her hand from his arm.

"I forgive ye," he whispered.

"Daniel, if you don't mind me asking, how'd you get those scars on your wrists?"

He stepped forward and they resumed their walk toward James Earl's home.

"I wuz put in irons on several occasions when I wuz a young man."

"Why?"

"Many reasons, I suppose. Mostly, my master wuz afraid of me. And he wuz afraid I'd run away. Funny thing is, them chains actually made me stronger. They be a bit heavy."

Lizzy considered the irony—the very item a man used to keep another man weak had actually strengthened him. "Was it hard?"

"I seen worse but, yes, after I turned fifteen it wuz much worse."

Daniel unlocked the front door. For an old man, James Earl kept a pretty clean house, Lizzy mused. "Show me the kitchen."

"Back here."

She watched Mo duck going through each doorway. *How tall is he?* Lizzy found a few small pans but nothing that would allow them to fix food for a crowd. "I'll need to bring some pots and pans over."

"I can help."

"Thank you, I might take you up on it. Daniel, who's paying for James's funeral?"

"I am, but don't go tellin' no one. It ain't something a man should speak about."

"You can afford it?"

"I have some money set aside. Been savin' for awhile."

"Saving for what?" she asked and sat in the caned chair next to the small kitchen table.

Daniel pulled up another and sat beside her.

"Don't rightly know, really. My momma told me to save as much money as I could. So I save. I suppose it will come in handy if I ever git married."

"Have you found someone?" Lizzy didn't know why she was asking. Perhaps all that marrying talk that Bea, her mother, and she were engaged in earlier.

"No, I cain't say that I has."

Lizzy found herself relieved that no one special was in Daniel's life. Not that she wanted to be the someone special. But somehow she was pleased to know there was no one.

She looked around the room, needing to change the subject. It was her own fault for bringing up such silly conversation. "This is a nice place. Who do you suppose owns it?"

"I do."

"What?" Lizzy peered into his midnight eyes. Oh, a woman could get lost in those eyes.

"James left it to me in his will."

"That's quite a gift."

"I don't know what I be doin' with a house."

Lizzy wanted to scream, *You could give it to me!* But that hardly seemed right or fair. "How many rooms does it have?"

"I don't know. Never counted."

"You could rent rooms, earn a little extra income."

"Perhaps. I don't fancy doin' other people's laundry. Where I rent, they wash my sheets once a week."

"Must be nice." Lizzy chuckled. "I do more laundry than any woman ought to. Four children of my own and their linens, plus my own, keep me hopping. Of course, Clarissa and I do everyone's together—goes faster with the two of us."

"You have a nice home, Lizzy."

"It belongs to my mother. But she's going to give it to George. I don't fit there, Daniel. I need my own place. A place to raise my family. I just can't afford it yet."

"On the plantation we would have as many as ten to a house as small as this room. That's needin' your own place."

"You know how to humble a gal." Was she just being selfish? She knew plenty of folks who had it worse off than she. She shared a room with her girls, the boys shared a room with George Jr., and George and Clarissa had their own room. Their daughters had her mother's old room.

"Miss Lizzy. . ."

"Just 'Lizzy' is fine."

Mo nodded. "Lizzy, would ye do me another favor?"

"Sure, if I can."

Mo reached into his pocket and pulled out an envelope. "James left this for me, next to the will. I wuz wonderin' ifin ye could read it."

"Sure."

"I tried, but he wrote different letters than ye taught me."

Lizzy opened her hand, palm side up, to receive the letter. After opening it, she commented, "Cursive. That's the type of lettering this is. What I'm teaching you is printing, and it's the style of letters for books, newspapers, and such. Cursive is what folks write letters to each other with."

"Why?"

Lizzy chuckled. "I don't know."

Mo wagged his head. "So many things don't make sense to me."

"You're not alone on that score." The handwriting was poor but legible. Lizzy cleared her throat and began to read.

Dear Daniel,

If you're reading this then I'm dead. Don't grieve, Son.

Lizzy paused. "James Earl was your father?"

"No. He just sort of adopted me."

"Oh, sorry." Lizzy continued.

I'm giving you the house in hopes you can use it one day to raise a family. As you know, my Emma and I, we didn't have no children. And I don't have no kin. No real kin. My father was white, my mother one of his slaves. When I grew to be a man, my father bought me this house and asked me never to return to the Bahamas. I was an embarrassment, you might say. He gave me and my mother our freedom and I stole my wife from him. To give you this house is to break the bondage of the past. A free man, with a free house. Find a wife, Mo, and fill the house with children. Don't mourn too long. I'm an old man. And I had a good life. Now, I'm joined with Emma again.

Your friend,
James

Lizzy wiped a tear from her eye. "He was a good friend, Daniel."

Mo fought the tightness in his throat. "Yes, he wuz." *But why didn't he tell me about his past? Why the big secret?* Even in the letter, James never revealed the man's name.

Lizzy folded the letter and placed it back in the envelope. "Here, you'll want to keep this."

Mo's hand trembled as he reached out for the letter. Lizzy grasped his hand with both of hers. He stood, pulling her up with him and embraced her. He needed to connect with someone. He needed her friendship, her warmth, her love.

seven

The weekend passed quickly. James Earl's funeral service and burial had taken up Lizzy's free time. She was happy to help, though, and so were others, once they learned of James Earl's death. For an old man, he had many acquaintances but few who were close friends.

The next few weeks went by uneventfully. On more than one occasion, Lizzy found herself thinking about James Earl's home and just how large it was. It had three bedrooms, a sitting room, a dining room, and a kitchen. She had to fight envying Daniel's possessions.

More and more women were warming up to Daniel on Sunday mornings at church. Her feelings of jealousy were another sin she had to fight. After all, she wasn't in love with Daniel, and she certainly wasn't looking to be falling in love with him—or anyone.

And just when she thought she had handed her sins to God, she remembered the embrace she had shared with Daniel in James Earl's kitchen. To be wrapped in Daniel's strong and protective arms would get any woman weak in the knees.

Lizzy brushed off her thoughts and continued to do the Sanchez's laundry. She'd taken home some of Mr. Sanchez's white shirts that needed ironing.

"Momma," William yelled, as he ran into the room.

"William, lower your voice. You're not outside. There's no need for yelling in the house."

"Yes, Ma'am." William lowered his head. The poor boy had such a thin body and such large hands and feet. She knew one day he'd be tall, possibly as tall as Daniel. *No,* she thought, *no one was as tall as Daniel!*

"Now, what's the matter?"

"Nothin'."

Lizzy blew out an exasperated breath. "Then what on earth were you yelling for?"

"Oh, Mr. Mo is coming with a wooden crate in his arms, and he says it's full of surprises."

What could he possibly be bringing over here? She placed the iron on the stove and reached the front room as Daniel entered carrying the wooden crate.

"Evenin', all. I'm come bearin' gifts."

"What's this?" Lizzy pointed to the crate.

"I wuz doin' some cleanin' in James's house and found some things I cain't use and thought the children might enjoy."

A circle of enraptured children gathered around Mo, each trying to sneak a peek at the items in the crate, and each trying to be patient and wait. Lizzy chuckled seeing young Henry, George's youngest, reaching out for the crate.

Daniel sat down on the sofa and placed the crate in front of him. "Now, let's see." He slowly lifted the cloth hiding the contents, building the children's curiosity.

"Vanessa." He reached his hand in, then pulled it out, continuing to explain. "I found this here book and thought ye might be interested in it. I think thar are some of the stories ye like readin' in thar."

"Oh, Mr. Mo, thank you." Vanessa cradled the book close to her chest and then she reached over and gave him a hug.

"Now, let's see, what have I got here?"

Lizzy smiled, watching the children lean slightly forward.

"Well, the next gift is for a man, and since none of ye fit that yet, I guess I better pass it over." Daniel winked at Lizzy.

She placed her hand over her grin so the children wouldn't see her laughing at them. All four boys' smiles slipped. Daniel continued, "Of course, someday some of ye will become men."

Benjamin straightened to his full height, followed by

George, then Henry. William, who didn't understand, tried to peer inside the crate.

"I reckon since Ben is the oldest. . ."

"But I'm only a month younger than him," George protested.

Daniel scratched his chin. "Hmm, well, we might have a problem here. 'Cept that I know one of you loves the ocean and being on boats."

"That be Ben. I can't swim." George slumped his shoulders.

"All right then, Ben, this here gift is for ye. It's a sextant, and the sailors use it to navigate their ships."

"Oh boy, Ma, look!" Benjamin brought his prize over to her for closer examination.

"It's wonderful, Ben. Don't you think you ought to thank Mr. Greene?"

"Sorry. Thank you, Sir." Ben went over and shook Daniel's hand. Lizzy grinned. He was trying to be such a man. But Daniel didn't settle for that and pulled the boy to him, giving him a big bear hug.

"Now, George, I do has something fer ye."

Daniel again fished through the crate. Lizzy noticed he pulled out a strange figurine. "James told me this is a soldier from the Far East. He said these soldiers were called samurai and were the best soldiers in their country. He also said this type of porcelain came from Japan as well. I don't know much about Japan 'cept what James said, and he didn't know much but the soldier was a man of honor, truthful, and a protector. Would ye like it?" Daniel gently handed the fine porcelain piece to George. "Be careful; it's very delicate," Daniel warned. "It's the kind of thing that best goes on a shelf where one looks at it and imagines."

George's hands trembled as they cupped to receive his new treasure. Lizzy made a mental note to learn what she could about Japan and add it to the child's lessons.

"Now, Sarah, I'm afraid James—not being a lady—didn't leave much to choose from, but I did find some things that belonged to James's wife, Emma. What I have here is a fine, bone china teacup with a matching dish. They's come from England, and when I saw the purty flowers on it, I thought of ye."

"Oh thank you, Mr. Mo, it's beautiful." Sarah hugged Daniel and kissed him on the cheek.

Daniel gave William a spin-top and Henry some glass marbles. And for Olivia he'd found a small, handmade doll with black button eyes. Each child thanked him and ran off to play with the new gifts.

"That was very special, Daniel. Thank you." Lizzy smiled.

"You're welcome. I don't have use fer those things and I figured the young'üns would enjoy 'em."

"You truly made their day."

Daniel bent down and reached into the crate. "I want ye to have this, Lizzy."

"Oh my, Daniel, it's beautiful." Lizzy held up a glass vase.

"When I saw it, I thought of ye. The colors are so rich and they change in the light. They remind me of yer eyes."

Lizzy blushed. "Thank you."

For the past few weeks she'd been fighting her growing attraction to Daniel. His kind and gentle way was wearing down her resolve not to get involved with another man. What frustrated her were times like this when he'd compliment her but wouldn't go further. *Does he care for me as a man cares for a woman? Or is he just being his typical, kind self?* Lizzy fought down her frustrations and asked, "Can I get you a drink?"

"No, thank ye. I need to get back to cleaning."

"I understand. Are you all moved in and settled?"

"I guess. I don't have much. I'm still havin' trouble livin' in James's home. Somehow it still doesn't feel right."

Lizzy reached out and placed her hand on his forearm. "It'll get better in time."

"I reckon youse is right."

Daniel moved, breaking her connection with him. He bent down and lifted the near-empty crate. "Oh, I almost forgot.

Give these to George and Clarissa."

He handed her a linen table cloth and a spy glass.

"You're sure you don't want these things?"

"Nah, don't have use fer 'em. Someone else should have the pleasure. Good day, Lizzy."

"Good-bye, Daniel." Lizzy found herself wanting to leap in his arms the way Olivia had and snuggle into his chest. To be wrapped in his arms again. . . She stopped her thoughts abruptly, brushed the heat from her face, and said, "God bless you, Daniel."

❧

Mo cradled the crate under one arm. He'd come bearing gifts just so he could get a glimpse of Lizzy. Why hadn't he accepted her invitation for a cold drink? Why couldn't he admit to her that he enjoyed her company? Why couldn't he allow himself to forget the past, the pain?

"Caron," he moaned. Had she really loved him? Or had she just seen him as a good man to have as a husband? He'd never know. He'd never return to the plantation to find out. She'd made her choice, and her choice wasn't him.

"Could Lizzy be interested in me as a man, Lord? I saw her blush. Can I be a good father to four children? I never had a father. . . I'm not sure what a man should do. Ahh, these be just silly thoughts, Lord. Sorry to bother Ye."

Mo decided to work in the yard. He needed good hard physical labor. He wanted to put in a small garden in the back for vegetables. Flowers would be pretty for the front, but those were extra. Food would be best. It was getting to the hottest months, so he didn't know which foods to plant; he'd have to ask around. One thing he enjoyed about Mr. Ellis's home was the various fruit trees. Mo thought he'd like to plant banana, passion fruit, and coconut palm trees first. He worked hard, digging and hoeing, getting the small patch of earth ready for some planting.

❧

Days later he found himself back at Lizzy's for his scheduled lesson. Reading children's books had a way of humbling a man, but he began to feel good about what he was accomplishing.

"Excellent, Daniel. You're really catching on quickly."

Mo's heart thumped in his chest. It meant more to him to make her proud than it did to actually have achieved anything in his reading and writing. "Thank ye."

"Daniel." She reached across the table and picked up a small leather-bound book. "I'd like to give you this."

He reached for the thick book and read the words. "A Bible?"

"It's a gift."

The dim light of the lamp darkened her hazel eyes. Their twinkling green rays captivated him.

"Daniel, I have other books to share with you. The works of former slaves like yourself. Frederick Douglass and William Wells Brown. But when I was reading over them they just didn't seem like the right pieces of literature to learn to begin reading. I mean, they bring the anger out in me; I can't imagine them not bringing the anger and memories out in you."

He glanced down at the Holy Word in his hand. His fingers followed the leather binding of the book, its ribbed edges and fine gold leaf lettering, worn over the years, but sparkling as if they were fresh golden hay glistening in the sun. His own book. His first book.

Lizzy continued, "I also have some older books written by black authors—poetry from Phillis Wheatley and Jupiter Hammon. But poetry is harder to comprehend. That's why I settled on God's Word. It'll be difficult in some places, but the truth will also minister to you as well."

His voice caught. "Thank ye, Lizzy."

"You're welcome. Take it home. Read what you can, and we'll discuss it next time."

He stood up, still stunned by the thoughtfulness of the gift. *My own Bible.*

She took back the Bible for a moment and opened it a few pages from the beginning. "Start reading here."

"G E N. . ." he began to spell out the larger word on the top of the page.

"Genesis," she supplied.

Mo smiled and repeated. "Genesis. Thank ye, Lizzy."

"In the beginning," he continued to read out loud. He paused and looked at the pleasure in her eyes. "Ye is a fine teacher, Lizzy."

She placed her hand lightly on his. "You're a fine student, Daniel. I've not had a finer."

Daniel felt his chest swell with pride. He never considered himself a vain man, but when Lizzy complimented him, he felt an overwhelming need to do even better the next time. "I must be going. Mr. Ellis needs me before the sun rises tomorrow."

She led him to the door. "Good night, Daniel."

"Good night, Lizzy." He fought off the desire to kiss her on the cheek, to thank her for such a generous gift. He knew his feelings for her were developing beyond simple friendship, and he didn't trust his reasons for wanting to kiss her. He stepped into the cool dark air and waved.

Daniel gazed into the night sky of black velvet peppered with sparkling white stars. A ring of midnight blue encircled the moon. "Oh, Lord, ye be a mighty fine painter tonight."

eight

Lizzy cuddled up beside Sarah as the gentle pink and purple hues of predawn sunlight filtered through her screened window. She brushed the soft curls away from her daughter's face. Sarah stirred in her arms. Her eyes slowly fluttered open. "Morning, Momma."

"Good morning, Sweetheart."

"Do I hafta stay with Aunt Clarissa today?"

"You know you do. What's the matter?"

"Nothing. It's just that I'd like to spend more time with you. Vanessa just reads all day, and Liv plays with Henry and William. Ben and George are always off doing boy stuff like catching lizards and snakes. Aunt Clarissa is all right, but she's got to work in the kitchen and around the house. A girl can only spend so long in the kitchen."

Lizzy suppressed a giggle. Her poor daughter didn't know the half of how long a woman actually spends in the kitchen. "I see—so you're by yourself most of the time."

Sarah nodded. She was Lizzy's quieter child. If any child could really be described as quiet, Sarah fit the bill. Lizzy sighed. "As much as I'd love to bring you with me to work, I'm afraid I simply can't do it. Mr. Sanchez has rules."

"I know, Momma, I just wished you didn't have to work. Liv doesn't like it either."

"And neither do I. But the good Lord decided I needed a job to help take care of you since your daddy passed. So I should do it the best I can."

Sarah snuggled closer. "Why did Daddy have to die?"

"I don't know, Child. I really don't know." Lizzy felt her stomach tighten. She wished she had the answers. Truth be told, she was still working on finding them for herself. She pulled Sarah close to her heart. "I love you, Princess."

"I love you too, Momma."

"I miss you too," Lizzy sympathized.

Sarah's head nodded up and down on her chest.

Oh, Lord, I know You have a plan, but I'm fresh out of answers. I wish I understood why You took Benjamin when You did. I know it was a bullet that killed him, and war is something You don't cotton to, but—leaving me with four young'uns. . . It just doesn't seem fair.

"Momma, what are we studying today when you come home from work?" Sarah pushed away from her mother's chest and looked at her from deep toffee eyes, her father's eyes.

Lizzy closed her eyes for a moment and pictured Ben and how proud he had been to go and fight for the cause. The war was won and now she could teach her children to read and write and not be afraid of being arrested. *You helped do that, Ben.* She whispered a prayer of thanks.

She opened her eyes and met her daughter's imploring gaze. "I think today we'll take a picnic and play at the beach."

"No schoolin'?" Sarah bounced up in the bed.

Lizzy chuckled. "No schooling."

Sarah embraced her with a big hug. Her bouncing woke Olivia. In moments Lizzy found herself being danced around by two gentle sprites, happy with life, happy to be alive.

Taking in a deep breath and letting it out slowly, she recommitted herself to moving forward with her life. For the sake of the children, for the sake of the cause. Her children would be smarter than her; her grandchildren would be even more educated. In the end, she believed, a Negro would have as much education as a white person and the freedom to rejoice in it.

❧

Mo dove into the crystal blue water. Everything on and around Key West seemed cleaner, purer, so incredibly different than plantation life. The muddy brown water of the Mississippi with its swirling eddies were like the pits of despair, nothing like the transparent blue seas of the tropical island. The fish in their brilliant colors danced in the sea, unlike the dark brown and black bottom-feeding catfish of the Mississippi. Even the birds here wore vivid colors of reds, yellows, and greens, while on the plantation he had seen only brown barn swallows. . . . He reached for the sponge with his left hand, lifted it slightly, and cut it from the coral reef with the knife in his right.

He rarely dove in and cut the sponges now, but the need to enjoy the warm water and the beauty of God's creation drove him through its cleansing waves. With enough air in his lungs, he cut additional sponges. A strong kick of his legs brought his head through the surface of the water. He gulped in some fresh air and dove again, filling the net hitched to his waist with sponges. The net full, he swam up to the skiff and climbed aboard.

Once in port, he unloaded the boat and set the sponges in the fresh water vat.

"Good haul, Mo." Ellis slapped him on the back.

"Thank ye, Sa."

"Did you want to go over the ledgers again this afternoon?"

If Ellis was asking if he wanted to, as in really looking forward to getting into his books, the answer was no. "Sure," Mo said.

Ellis chuckled. "Such enthusiasm."

"I's not sure I'll ever understand dem books."

"You will. You already recognize all the words on the columns."

"Yes, Sa, but I'm thinkin' my mind ain't made for addin' and subtractin'."

He'd been trying to learn Ellis's books for months now. *It sure didn't take this long to learn to read from Miss Lizzy.*

Ellis roared with laughter. "Come on."

Mo put his shirt back on and headed into the small building at the end of the wharf. Ellis stood in the center with his hands on his hips. "You know, I think I'm going to build another building at the end of the dock on shore. We need more room."

"Want me and the men to help build it?"

"Possibly." Ellis scratched his beard. "Need to think on it for a bit."

Mo placed the ledger on top of the small desk.

"How's the house coming along?" Ellis moved to the desk, sat on the stool beside it, and grabbed a pen.

"Fine, fine. Most of the extra things a man don't need I've given away. The garden is in; top soil ain't too thick."

"It isn't like the North." Ellis placed his hand on a set of figures.

"Mr. Mo! Mr. Mo!" Benjamin came running up the dock.

"Benjamin?" Trailing behind him was George. "What's the matter?"

"I'm not sure. Momma came home in tears. I've never seen her this way. Uncle George and Aunt Clarissa went to Key Visca. They won't be back till tomorrow. I didn't know who else to come to, 'cept you and Mr. Ellis." Benjamin nodded toward Ellis as he stepped out of the shed.

"May I leave, Mr. Ellis?" Mo turned to his boss.

"Please—find out what's wrong. Have one of the boys come back and tell me if everything is all right."

Mo nodded and made it to shore in a dozen large steps.

"Wait for me," Benjamin cried.

Daniel stopped. *Lord, I don't know what's wrong with Lizzy, but please help me to be able to help her.*

❧

Lizzy locked her bedroom door and flung herself on the bed. Tears burned her cheeks. "How dare he!" she fumed. She threw a pillow across the room, hitting a picture frame so that it hung crooked on the wall.

"Momma, are you all right?" Sarah knocked on the door.

"I'm fine, Honey. I just need to be alone for a few minutes." She knew she wasn't convincing anyone, least of all her children, who knew her better than anyone else. How could she hide this evil from them? How could she provide for them? She couldn't go back to work. *Not now. Not there.*

Lizzy's heart wrenched deep inside. She cradled another pillow to her chest. What was she going to do?

Certainly not what Mr. Sanchez wants, she determined, bolstering her resolve. But how could she go back to that house, knowing what he wanted, knowing she was putting her very virtue at risk. He'd nearly assaulted her this morning.

Her mind flashed back to his hot breath on her neck, his arms. . . Shaking her head to remove the images, she tightened her grasp around the pillow. Olivia's pillow. Her daughter's pure scent filled her nostrils. She breathed in deeply, holding in the memory of her daughter, her innocence. Her sweet daughter.

"Oh, God, help me. Why? Why? Why did he have to do this?" She curled up into a ball.

❧

Mo entered the house and found the group of children huddled around Lizzy's bedroom door.

"Mr. Mo," Sarah sniffled, wiping a tear from her eye.

"Is she in there?" Of course she was in there. He needed to help the children calm down. He needed to calm down. "Tell me what happened."

Olivia ran to him and hugged his legs. He leaned down and picked her up. "She's goin' to be okay." He prayed his words were true. "Come on, children, let's do something special for yer Momma."

"What?" William whispered. His thin little limbs shook with fear.

"I say we make a fancy dinner for her and set the table up real special like."

"How?" George Jr. asked.

"By picking some flowers to put on the table. William, ye and Henry are in charge of gettin' the flowers. Ben, ye and George can go to town and git me some things for supper." Mo reached into his pocket and pulled out some coins. "Vanessa, ye and Sarah can help in the kitchen."

"You know how to cook?" Sarah knitted her eyebrows.

"Not like yer mother, but I can do a fair job."

Olivia clung to his neck. "Liv, you'll set the table. Let's see, what should we have fer supper?" He tapped his foot and looked up at the ceiling, then peeked a glance at the children. It was working; he was getting their attention on him and less on Lizzy.

"I know," he squatted down to meet the children's gaze. "Word is, a new shipment of beef came in from Cuba today. Why don't we fetch some?"

The children all nodded their heads. "Okay, boys, you're in charge of getting the meat. Girls, put on some rice and beans. William, Henry, don't forget the flowers."

They all ran to their appointed tasks.

After a few minutes Olivia slid out of his arms and began putting the plates on the table. Holding a plate in two hands, she looked up. "Momma was going to take us on a picnic today."

"I'm sure she'll take ye another day."

Olivia placed the plate down and put her hands on her hips. She sucked in her lower lip and wrinkled her forehead, lifting one eyebrow. "I think you're right." She removed her hands from her hips and stepped to the sideboard to retrieve another plate. "I don't like it when mommas are sick."

"I don't like it either, Sweetheart. Why don't I go and see if yer Ma needs anythin'?"

"I think that be good, Mr. Mo." Olivia put another plate on the table. A grin inched up his cheek.

Mo slipped down the hall and tapped the bedroom door with his knuckle.

He paused and listened. He waited.

No response.

He tapped again a little louder. Again he waited.

Again no response.

He tapped again and spoke softly, "Lizzy, it's me, Daniel."

He heard her moan. His stomach twisted inside. Should he open the door? Should he give her more time?

"Lizzy, may I come in?" He heard the bed creak.

nine

Oh, Lord, I can't face Daniel. Not now, not like this. Please, send him away.

"Lizzy, speak to me or I'm gonna open this door."

She heard him check the doorknob.

"Lizzy, I'll break down the door. Speak to me." His voice became firmer, more determined.

She closed her eyes and pictured him standing on the other side of the door. A smile touched her lips at the thought of him shifting his huge frame against her door. She couldn't picture anything withstanding a direct assault from Daniel.

"Lizzy?" His voice raised another notch. "Last warning."

"Daniel, no. I'm fine."

"Ye ain't fine. But I'll not push ye fer more. I'm just letting ye know that in about an hour the children are putting together a dinner fer ye. Something special. Will ye be ready to come out by then?"

"I–I. . . ," she whispered.

"Lizzy?"

She heard him grumble and stomp off. Lizzy took in a deep breath. At least she didn't have to face him right now. What should she tell him? She curled back into the fetal position on the bed, hugging Olivia's pillow again. Her thoughts drifted to Sarah. Was it just this morning when she awoke with no fears, enjoying her daughter, the day, life?

The distant sound of scraping metal tickled her ears. What was that? What were they doing out there? Lizzy sat up on the bed just as her bedroom door opened.

"Lizzy?" Mo stood in her doorway.

She flung Sarah's pillow at him. He simply stood there, not catching it, not picking it up. Nothing.

"What happened, Lizzy? Are ye all right?" he asked.

Lizzy could feel her entire body begin to shake.

In one large step Mo had crossed the room from the door to her bedside. He picked her up in his arms and cradled her. She wrapped her arms around his neck and cried into his shoulder.

He sat on the bed, still holding her in his arms, and rocked her. Setting her on his lap, he raised a hand and brushed the tears from her face. "No one. . ." His voice faltered. "No one. . . took liberties with ye?" he asked.

She shook her head no. But could she tell him that Mr. Sanchez had wanted to?

He rocked her some more. She felt like a child again, sitting in her father's lap. All the comfort, love, and security her father had for her she felt coming from Daniel.

She heard Benjamin yell, "Mr. Mo, we got some beef."

"Bring it to the kitchen," Mo called back to them. "I don't want to leave ye like this, Lizzy," he whispered against her arm.

"I'll be all right." She sniffed.

"Ye take some more time to yourself. The children and I have everything under control. If ye come to dinner, it'll mean a lot to the children. But ifin ye can't, I can explain it to them. I'll have the older ones take care of the younger ones with regard to getting them ready for bed after dinner. But after those young'uns are settled, youse and me is goin' to have a talk. I don't know what happened, but I'm fightin' all sorts of horrible images in my mind. I told Olivia ye probably didn't feel well. They need answers, Lizzy. They're scared. I'll help, but they need their mother to tell them everythin' is goin' to be all right."

"I'll come out for dinner."

"Good." Daniel lifted her up off of his lap and placed her on the bed.

He lifted me like I was no more than a ten-pound sack of flour, she mused. She reached for his arm. "Thank you."

He took her hand with his and tenderly kissed it. "You're welcome."

❧

He released her hand, cherishing the tender trail her fingers left as they pulled away from his. *Goodness, Lord, I'm gettin' mighty strong feelin's fer this woman. I just don't know if I can be a father to four children. And no man ought to awaken desire in a woman ifin he cain't take on her young'uns as his own.* Daniel closed the door behind him. He found the older boys were sitting in the living room.

Benjamin had his arms crossed and his hands hitched up under his armpits. *The poor fellow probably doesn't know what to do with himself.*

"How is she?" Ben asked.

"Better. She asked fer a few more minutes." Daniel came over and placed a hand on the boy's shoulder. "She's goin' to be just fine."

"What happened?" Ben pushed.

"I don't know, but I suspect someone said somethin' to hurt her feelings."

George jumped up. "Who? I'll go take care of 'em."

He couldn't fault the boy for having the same feelings as himself. "Ye set yourself right down in that chair. I knows your mom and dad didn't teach you to fight first."

George hung his head. "No, Sir," he mumbled.

"Look boys, ye bein' the oldest boys, I'm goin' to need yer help. I ain't never had no young'uns, and I'm not sure what to do, so can ye help me?" Both boys stood taller, puffed out their chests, and gave him a nod. "Why don't ye see if Olivia needs any more help settin' the table."

They scurried off and Daniel glanced at Lizzy's door. Tonight ought to be a good test as to whether or not he could take on the responsibility of another man's children. It wasn't that he didn't love children or that he didn't already feel a bond to Lizzy's children. He just wasn't sure what a man should do to help raise a child. Being a slave took away your rights to your children. You could be sold, or your children sold, with no say in the matter. *We was property, Lord. Just plain old property. At times we didn't even feel human.* Mo fought the bile rising in his stomach. "Chattel, Lord, nothing but chattel," he muttered out loud.

"What's chattel, Mo?" William asked, as he entered the house carrying an array of bright red, orange, and yellow flowers.

"It's the name for what the white slave owners call their slaves. It means property."

"What's property?" William stood beside him.

Daniel squatted down beside the boy and placed his hand on the boy's shoulder. His innocent brown eyes bore into him. A free child. A boy that will never know slavery. *Thank Ye, Lord, fer that.*

"Property is something ye own. Like yer shoes and clothes."

"So being a slave means someone owns you?"

"Yes." Daniel's throat tightened.

"My daddy went to fight to free the slaves."

"Your daddy wuz a brave man."

William nodded. "Mr. Mo, why do you have scars on your wrists?"

The boy didn't know half of his scars. Mo had caught a glimpse of his own back once in a mirror and winced at the sight. "I wuz in chains from time to time as a slave."

"Why?"

"Mostly 'cause my master seemed mighty afraid of me."

"Why?"

Daniel chuckled. "Well, 'cause I'm a big man, and I'm a very dark man."

"But you don't scare me," William protested.

"Thank ye, Son." Mo rubbed the top of William's head. "We best put dem flowers in some water or they won't be lookin' so nice for yer Momma."

"Mr. Mo," Vanessa called.

Maybe tonight's more of a warnin' that I cain't handle a

pack of young'uns. Mo rose from his squatted position and headed into the kitchen.

"I'm not sure how you want to cook this meat." Vanessa spread her hand over a large hunk of red and white marbled beef.

"George, where did the butcher say this here meat came from?" Mo asked.

George peeked around the corner. "Said it was from the rump. Called it a rump roast."

"Thanks." Daniel looked over the thick hunk of beef. It was too late to cook it in an oven, or even on a spit over an open fire. "Let me have the knife." He reached his hand out and she placed a large knife with a wooden handle in his hand.

"Let's make steaks. I'll cut up the meat and ye can fry 'em in the pan."

"All right. Should I season it?" Vanessa asked.

"Yes. Salt, pepper, and sauteed onions and garlic, if ye have some."

"I can cut up some green onions," Sarah offered.

"Sounds wonderful." Mo sliced the beef into inch-thick slabs. "These left over pieces can be put into a pot for some soup tomorrow." Mo gathered a small pile of ends and tips of the meat. "Or they can be dried."

"I'll ask Aunt Lizzy after she comes out." Vanessa placed her tiny hand on his. "Is she okay?"

"Yes, she'll be fine."

Vanessa nodded her head and went right to work frying up the steaks.

"Smells delicious." Lizzy entered the kitchen and winked at him. "Daniel, you didn't tell me you knew how to work in a kitchen."

"Been on my own for a few years. A man learns to cook or he starves."

Lizzy chuckled. "You ought to get yourself a wife."

Mo felt his face grow warm. He was thankful that his skin's dark tones would not reveal too much.

"Momma, I cut the onions," Sarah boasted.

"And you did a mighty fine job, too." Lizzy hugged her daughter.

"Are you feeling better, Momma?"

Daniel watched the interchange between mother and daughter. *Lizzy's a good mother*, he silently praised.

"Yes, Sweetheart. I'm much better now."

"What happened?"

"Someone said some bad things to me."

"I'm sorry, Momma. Jesus says we're not to say bad things. Maybe the bad person doesn't know Jesus."

"You may be right, Child."

"Aunt Lizzy, I'm frying steaks." Vanessa smiled.

"I thought I smelled something wonderful. Where'd we get the beef?"

George and Benjamin walked in. "We got it."

Lizzy caught Daniel's gaze and mouthed a silent thank you. He smiled back. "Fine shoppers, these boys. Came home with a rump roast."

"Rump, huh?" Lizzy giggled.

"Well, it sounds a lot better than buttocks." Daniel grinned. It was wonderful seeing the tension ease. In the corner of Lizzy's eyes he saw the strain. She was putting up an excellent front, a front for her children. Tonight would take all of his self-control, he knew. Once she told him what he suspected, he would need every ounce of his strength to keep himself planted in the room and not find the person, probably a man, who had mistreated her.

"Eww," Henry groaned. "I ain't eating somebody's buttocks."

"Nope, you'll be eating steak."

"Oh, okay. Who said it was buttocks?" The room erupted into laughter.

❧

Lizzy watched Daniel as he worked with the children. They all seemed genuinely enamored with him. He sat on the chair and allowed them to climb on him or huddle close to him. Dinner had been wonderful. The children had gone out of their way to be perfect ladies and gentlemen. Lizzy sighed. Daniel and the children in the chair were living shadows of what her life would have been like if Ben hadn't been killed in the war.

She knew Mr. Sanchez would never have made his rude suggestion if Ben hadn't died. Lizzy felt her blood rise a notch. She didn't want to tell Daniel, and yet she figured he probably guessed what must have happened.

Lizzy recalled being in Daniel's tender embrace. So gentle, so kind, so. . .loving? Daniel? She shook the thought off. He'd have been that way with anyone. Wouldn't he?

She snatched a glimpse of his mahogany eyes, his rugged chin, and wonderfully full lips. Lips? What on earth was she doing looking at his lips? She dropped her gaze immediately.

The hour was late and she needed to put the children to bed. On the other hand, if she put them to bed, she'd have to discuss the day's events with Daniel. But she'd put off sending them to bed long enough. "It's that time."

"Oh, Momma," four of them whined. The other three simply moaned, "Do we hafta?"

"Yes. Now, go get yourselves ready and I'll be in to say your prayers with each of you. Scoot."

"Good night, Mr. Mo." Olivia reached up and hugged him, giving him a kiss on the cheek.

"Good night, Mr. Mo," the chorus chimed in. Each gave him a hug and kiss. She watched his eyes pool with unshed tears. For a tree-trunk of a man, he had the most tender heart she'd ever seen.

"Good night, young'uns. Ye did a mighty fine job tonight. I'm mighty proud of y'all."

They each beamed from his praise.

"Momma, can Mr. Mo say our prayers with us?" William asked.

Lizzy glanced back at Daniel. "Would you like to?"

"I'd be honored."

"Mine too?" A chorus then ensued: "Me. . . Me. . . Me!"

Lizzy chuckled. "All right, if Mr. Mo is up for it."

Daniel grinned. "I think y'all is just tryin' to stay up a few extra minutes. But I'll come and listen to yer prayers. Shoo now."

The seven all ran to their rooms. Lizzy could hear them tossing their shoes and clothing off. "Thank you, Daniel."

"You're welcome. Why don't ye fix us some tea or hot cocoa while I git the little ones settled."

"Sure. You don't have to stay. I'm fine." She hoped he'd take the hint.

His eyes burrowed deep into her soul. "No, I don't think ye be fine yet. We need to talk, Lizzy. Ye need to tell someone."

"But. . ."

"Shh." He stepped up beside her and cradled her in his arms. Her defenses vanished. He was such a kind man. He'd understand. She hoped.

When Daniel released her, her knees wobbled. Maybe she did need his strength tonight. Maybe she should go see her mother. She'd know what to do. Perhaps Daniel would stay while the children slept so she could visit her mom.

Lizzy curled her lower lip and nibbled it. *Well, Lizzy old girl, you best be making the man some tea unless you're wanting to impose upon him some more.*

Mechanically, she worked her way around the kitchen. Water, tea kettle, stove, fire. . . She reminded herself what to do at each step. Then she stared off into space. Another kitchen came into focus.

Mr. Sanchez entered the room as she worked with Mrs. Sanchez's dress, pressing it, getting every wrinkle out.

"Lizzy, I know you're finding it hard to make ends meet."

A surge of joy entered her. Perhaps the Sanchezes knew of another family who needed some extra help around the house. "Yes."

"Well, I have a proposition for you." His smile tightened.

His gaze shifted down from her face to her bosom. Oh, God, no, please, stop him, Lord, she silently prayed. She grasped the iron more tightly as she counted the steps to the back door.

"Don't be frightened. I'm just offering you some extra income to be my mistress."

"No!" she protested.

"I won't hurt you, Lizzy. A man needs. . ."

"Lizzy?" Daniel's voice drew her from the memory. "Lizzy, are ye all right?"

"Oh, Daniel." She fell into his arms. "It was horrible. I said no. I told him no, several times."

"Did he take advantage of ye?"

"No, he just spoke such vile things. Things private between a husband and wife. I–I. . ."

"Who was it, Lizzy? I'll take care of him. He won't be sayin' anythin' like that to ye again," Daniel fumed.

ten

Daniel held Lizzy in his arms with all the tenderness he could muster. A part of him wanted to strike out so badly he could taste the coppery scent of blood. "Who, Lizzy?"

"No, Daniel. You can't; you'll be arrested."

"So, he wasn't Negro."

She tossed her head back and forth, saying "no" into his chest. He caressed her hair. It felt like fine wool already spun and ready for making a soft sweater.

"Who, Lizzy? He cain't get away with this."

"He didn't touch me. He tried but. . ."

The angry flames of justice burned more deeply in his chest. "Who, Lizzy?"

"No, Daniel. You'll be arrested. I can't allow that. I'm all right. He didn't touch me."

"No. It ain't right. A man should not take such liberties with a woman. Ye a free woman, not some slave given to her master's whims. I won't stand fer it. Tell me who, Lizzy."

Lizzy clutched his shirt. Her hot tears fell on his chest.

He cradled her more gently. "Shh. I won't push ye any further, Lizzy."

"Thank you, Daniel."

The tea kettle whistled.

"Come, let's have something to drink." He led her to the table. Somehow he needed to get her to talk with him. To confide in him. But pushing her obviously wouldn't work. *Help me, Lord.*

Lizzy left his arms and wrapped a cloth around the handle of the kettle. She poured the hot water into the earthen mugs and set some tea leaves on top.

Daniel rubbed the day-old growth on his chin. By this time

of night he usually shaved if he was going to be seeing folks in the evening. "If I promise not to beat the man mere inches from his life, will ye tell me who it is?"

"Daniel." She placed her hand on his. He grasped it, her long delicate fingers such a contrast to his own thick ones.

"It's just not right, Lizzy."

"No, it's not. But what can we do about it? Folks just think because of the color of our skin. . ."

"No, Lizzy, that's not true. It's taken me a lot of years to realize that, but I've seen good men and bad men, and they come in all colors."

"I suppose you're right. But. . ."

"Ye think he made the proposition just because ye were a Negro?"

"I don't know." She grasped her mug and spooned in some raw sugar cane. He did likewise. "Maybe he just thought I'd be easy."

"Maybe. But why do ye think that?"

" 'Cause he knows I need the money."

"He was offerin' to pay ye to, to. . ."

"Yes," she whispered.

Daniel clamped his jaw shut. What he was about to say wasn't pleasant, and he wasn't so sure he could keep the volume down so as not to wake the children. He contained his reactions and looked more closely at Lizzy. "Oh, Lizzy." He was beside her in seconds. The woman was trembling. "I promise not to hurt the man, and I'm sorry I'm more caught up in my own anger than seein' yer pain. Forgive me."

❧

Hot tears flowed down her cheeks. She couldn't believe Daniel was asking for forgiveness. He'd been a perfect gentleman. "Oh, Daniel, you've done nothing to be forgiven for."

"I put myself before ye. Ain't Christian."

She looped her arms around his strong and massive neck. He pulled her up and cradled her in his arms. She held him tighter. "I was going to ask you to stay with the children while I ran to see my mother."

"I don't want ye out on the streets like this, Lizzy. It ain't safe."

Lizzy swallowed. He was probably right.

"Lizzy, wuz it your boss, Mr. Sanchez?"

She tried to hide her reaction.

"I thought as much." He carried her into the living room and placed her on the sofa. "I'll walk ye to and from work. He'll see me and he won't try anythin' with ye."

"I can't ask you to do that."

"I cain't see ye goin' back to his house. He'll keep comin' and askin'. Can ye find another job?"

"No, I haven't been successful. The island's income hasn't been all that high since the beginning of the war. Not too many folks can afford to pay for extra staff."

"I don't like it, Lizzy. I'll need to come with ye. He won't touch ye, once he sees me."

Lizzy grasped his hands. "No, Daniel, he'll have you arrested. It's as you say—he'd be terrified of you. He'd find a reason to get you in trouble."

"Ye cain't arrest a man for nothin'."

"No, but I wouldn't put it past him to make up lies and say you did something you didn't do." As fair as the sheriff had been to Negroes, she still didn't trust him not to believe the opinion of another person over a black person. No, she couldn't put Daniel in harm's way just to protect her virtue.

"Then ye cain't return to work."

"I need the income."

"God will provide another job. Ye cain't go back."

"I have no choice, Daniel."

"Elizabeth Hunte, ye do have a choice. Youse a free woman; ye ain't a slave." If she wasn't going to allow him to walk her to and from work, then he'd have to see that she didn't go back to the job. He needed to protect her. He understood her need to provide for her family. In fact, it was one of the things that made her so special to him. *Yes, Lord, she is special to me*, he silently admitted.

Fresh tears streamed down her face.

"I knows what it's like to have no choice. But ye do, and God will provide."

"What do I tell Mrs. Sanchez? I—I just don't know what to do."

Daniel reached over and wrapped a protective arm around her shoulders. *She's so fragile, Lord. I needs to say the right thing. Help me.* "Lizzy, I can help with yer expenses until ye find a new job."

"I couldn't take your money, Daniel."

"Sure ye could. I don't need what I used to since James gave me his house."

"No, Daniel, it wouldn't be right."

It wasn't fair. No man should take advantage of a woman. He was fighting the urge to pay a midnight visit to Mr. Manuel Sanchez, but he'd given his word to Lizzy that he wouldn't beat the man. On the other hand, she probably was right that if Sanchez saw him, he'd call the sheriff and claim Mo had come looking for him. And what was Mo's connection to Lizzy other than friendship? It wasn't like he was her husband, and. . . "Lizzy, I've got it. Ye and I need to git married. Mr. Sanchez wouldn't dare lay a hand on ye ifin he knows ye is married to me. And the sheriff wouldn't be blaming a man fer protecting his wife."

"Marry you?"

"Yeah. Look, I have a big house, more room than a single man needs. I can provide fer ye and the children, Lizzy."

Lizzy pushed herself away from him. Her gaze locked with his. "You're asking me to marry you for my honor?"

"Yes. I guess I am." Did she not want to be married to a man such as himself? Perhaps his lack of education was a problem. "It wouldn't have to be a real marriage. I could be your husband in name only. You'd be protected."

"Let me get this straight. You're not offering me marriage out of love, just offering marriage for protection?"

"Yes." Daniel looked at her. *I'm missing something here. She's looking mighty angry, Lord.*

"No, Daniel. I can't marry you for that." Lizzy got up and walked across the room. "Daniel, I've had a long, hard day. Please don't take this the wrong way, but would you please leave?" Her voice was tight.

He rose from the sofa. "I'm sorry to have offended ye, Lizzy. I should have known." Silently he left her house.

Outside, he hurried off her property and ran toward the ocean. "Oh, God, I said it all wrong. I wuz just tryin' to help." He ripped off his shirt and flung his shoes down to the sand. He needed to work off his anger, his frustration. He dove into the ocean and began to swim. Long hard thrusts with his powerful arms and mighty kicks with his legs pulled him further and further from shore. Swimming at night in the tropics wasn't the wisest of choices, but he almost wished a barracuda would come after him so he could rip it apart with his bare hands.

❧

Lizzy gripped her sides. Not only had Mr. Sanchez propositioned her, but Daniel had decided to marry her, not out of love or romance, but just as an excuse to give him the right to walk her to work. Lizzy paced the front room back and forth. Each step brought renewed anger. She needed to talk with her mother, to someone, anyone. No, that wasn't true. She had talked with Daniel, and it only made her more upset than if she'd kept what had happened to herself. She was such a fool. *A man just doesn't understand, Lord.*

She looked out her side window to see if her neighbors still had a light on. A warm glow emanated from the back bedroom. *They're down for the night, but they aren't asleep yet.* Lizzy hurried over to their house and feverishly knocked on their door.

"Lizzy, what's the matter?" Mabel Jones clutched her nightclothes shut under her chin.

"I need a favor. I have to run and see my mother about

something. Could you sit with the children? George and Clarissa are away."

"Of course. Let me get my robe and I'll come right over."

"Thank you." Lizzy hurried back home. With seven kids it was always possible to have at least one wake up in the middle of the night.

Soon Mabel knocked on her front door.

"Thanks so much for coming."

"Are you sure you're all right?"

"Fine." Lizzy looked away from Mabel's imploring gaze. "I just need to speak with my mother."

Mabel reached out and touched her shoulder. "Lizzy, I don't know what happened, but your young'uns were all upset about your coming home crying. When I saw Mo Greene come over I figured you'd be all right. He didn't hurt you, did he?"

"Oh goodness, no. Daniel's as gentle as a lamb."

"Daniel?" Mabel's puzzled look spoke volumes.

"Sorry. Mo's given name is Daniel. I've found it fits him better than Mo. So I tend to call him Daniel."

Mabel nodded. "You go speak with your momma. If anyone can help you see straight it's Francine. God's given her a mighty fine gift to look right to the heart of a matter."

"Thanks for understanding. I'll be back as soon as I can. You can lay down on George and Clarissa's bed if you get tired," Lizzy offered.

"I might just do that. Now run along, Child, and be careful."

"I will, thanks."

Lizzy sprinted toward Ellis Southard's home. *Father, keep Mom awake for me. I need her, Lord.* She rounded the corner and saw a lamp burning in the front parlor. Relief washed over her.

She lightly knocked on the large oak door. Bea answered it. "Lizzy, what's the matter?"

"I need to speak with my mother," she explained, holding back her tears.

"Come in, come in. Are you all right?"

Lizzy nodded.

Bea wrapped her arm around Lizzy and led her to the front sitting room. "You sit down and I'll get Cook."

Bea walked down the hall toward Lizzy's mother's room. Lizzy could hear mumbling, followed by, "Lizzy?"

Without taking the time to put on a robe, her mother entered the sitting room in her nightclothes. "What's the matter to bring you out so late at night?"

"Oh, Mom." Fresh tears trailed down her cheeks. Francine came up beside her on the sofa and enveloped her with her ample arms. Bea brought in her mother's robe and whispered something about tea.

"Tell me what happened, Dear." Francine stood and put on her robe.

"Oh, Mom, it was horrible. Mr. Sanchez wanted to hire me to be his mistress. I've never felt so, so, sick in all my life. I've been working for them for years and he's never even looked at me in such a way. It just doesn't make sense."

"Of course it makes sense. 'Tis rude and unforgivable, but it makes sense. You're a widow, Lizzy. A beautiful widow. Men get to thinkin' you're lonely and will be easy."

"Easy!" Lizzy huffed. "If I'd done half the things my mind wanted to do to him, he would have no question I am not easy."

Francine chuckled. "No, I imagine not. Being propositioned comes with being a widow, I'm afraid. Men—not all, but some men—are full of sin, and they gets themselves in such bad ways they can't think straight."

"After Daddy died, did, did. . ."

"Of course, I had offers. Didn't have a mind to take anyone up on them. Those kind of men don't appeal to me. Besides, I'm older. I had far more years with George than you had with Ben."

"What am I going to do? I'm afraid to go back to work. Daniel said I shouldn't."

Francine raised her eyebrows.

"The children ran and got him when I came home crying."

"And Mr. Ellis ain't come home yet, had dinner and meetings in town this evenin' or else he would have told me and I would have come over. Curious, the children didn't fetch me."

"Actually, I believe they tried, but you weren't home."

"Must have been when I was in town doing some shopping. In fact, I thought I saw George and Benjamin buying some meat at the butcher's."

"Yeah, Daniel had the kids make me a special dinner. Vanessa fried up some steaks."

"Sounds nice. So is Daniel with the children now?"

Bea brought in a teapot and cups. "I won't intrude, but I thought you might like a cup of tea. And this."

Bea handed her a fine white handkerchief.

"Thanks. You can stay."

"Oh, good. Otherwise, I'd have to pump your mother full of questions after you left." Bea settled on a chair opposite the sofa.

Lizzy chuckled and quickly recounted Mr. Sanchez's vile offer.

"Mo knows?" her mother asked.

"Yes, but only after I made him promise not to kill the man. I don't want him being arrested trying to protect my honor. In fact, he wanted to walk me to work to put the fear of God into Mr. Sanchez."

"Sounds like a wise idea." Francine picked up her cup of tea.

"No, Mother, I can't let him do that. Mr. Sanchez might make up something so Daniel would end up in jail."

"Hmm, you might be right there."

"How could he?" Bea asked.

Lizzy looked at her mother. She loved Bea, but sometimes she didn't have a clue what it was like to be living in this world with dark skin. Bea didn't see skin color, and Lizzy cherished that about her.

"Because he's a very dark Negro. If Mr. Sanchez was

afraid enough of him, he might lie."

"But Mo can tell the sheriff the truth." Bea knitted her eyebrows. Then slowly raised them. "Oh, you mean. . ."

"Exactly."

"Oh." Bea bobbed her head up and down, finally comprehending.

"After I told Daniel no, he insisted I not go back to work. Jobs are hard to come by. I can't just leave it."

"But you're not safe there, Lizzy," Bea gasped.

"No, I suppose I'm not. But I don't know what to do." A nervous giggle slipped out her throat. "Daniel decided the next best thing was for me to marry him. Can you believe that?"

eleven

Back on shore, Mo lay on the beach and looked up at the stars. He was free, as free as the stars in the sky. But what was he free to do? He couldn't protect a woman for fear he'd be arrested. "It ain't right, Lord."

His mind shifted to messages he'd heard preached before, like when Stephen was stoned to death simply for telling others about Jesus. "Should I risk bein' arrested and confront Mr. Sanchez? Lord, I don't knows what to do. And why'd I make Lizzy mad all over again by askin' her to marry me? I have a home, plenty of room, and I think she likes me well enough. Am I so worthless that someone as pretty and wise as Lizzy couldn't find me worthy?"

Mo pulled in a deep breath that filled his lungs, raising his chest to its full size. "Ye know, Lord, being a big man has its problems. I've been whipped, beaten, and given up for dead a few times just 'cause of my size."

He scanned the sky to where a sliver of the moon pointed down to the sea. Following the direction of the moon's light, he looked over the inky black ocean. The horizon merged into the night. He knew the ocean carried on for miles, but the blanket of darkness hid the majestic wonder of the crystal blue sea. "Sure does look different from this morning, Lord."

Was it only this morning when he'd swum in the ocean without a care in the world? "Lord, I know Lizzy don't want me to walk her to work, but I hafta. I cain't let her go unprotected."

The muscles on his back tightened. His hand clenched. He wasn't about to let another woman whom he cared about get mistreated by someone. Not now. Not with him being a free man and able to stop it.

Mo brushed the sand from his body and picked up his shirt and shoes. He'd need to get to bed if he was going to wake up bright and early tomorrow morning. "First, Mr. Ellis will need to know I'm comin' into work late," he mumbled to himself. He walked past Lizzy's home. The house stood quiet. A dim light shown through the front window. He wanted to see her again, to try and explain why he'd offered marriage. But tomorrow morning would be soon enough. She needed more time to relax. Truth was, he knew he needed more time too. "She's a stubborn woman, Lord. Purty, but stubborn."

At his home, he lit a lamp in the kitchen, then headed outside to wash the salt from his body. After he dried himself off and headed into the house, he heard a noise in his bedroom. Mo reached for the large cast iron frying pan from the top of the stove and stealthily headed into the back room. He took a step, then stopped to listen, shifting his weight to his right foot.

The room was silent.

He moved forward again, shifting his weight to his left foot, and paused.

He heard a strangled cough.

"Who's in here?" he demanded.

❧

"Mo asked ye to marry him?" Francine slapped her knee and smiled. "That's wonderful, Dear. But I wasn't aware that the two of you had taken a shine to each other."

"There's no shine, Mom. The man offered marriage for protection. Protection!" her voice raised. "Can you imagine the gall?"

Bea giggled. "Some have married for less."

"I can't do it. It's just not right."

"Look at me, Child," Francine demanded. "Do you love him?"

"No. It's like I said, we're friends. At least, I think we're friends." Lizzy focused on her hands, folding and refolding the handkerchief.

"Ahh, but I'm thinkin' you've been thinkin' more about him," her mother pushed.

Lizzy felt the heat rise on her cheeks.

"Is it true, Lizzy? Have you started to have feelings for Mo?" Bea asked.

"No," she protested. "Oh, I don't know. I was looking at his lips tonight," she mumbled. Her cheeks flamed even brighter.

"So, you're more upset with Mo because he's offering marriage and isn't feelin' the same way about you." Francine crossed her arms over her ample chest and began to chuckle. "You do care for him, Lizzy. I can see it."

"I care, but I don't know if I love him. I'm just starting to have feelings for him. A woman shouldn't marry a man if she doesn't have feelings for him," she argued, defending her position and looking toward Bea for some help.

Bea raised her hands in surrender. "I'm not getting in the middle of Cook's matchmaking."

Lizzy groaned. "What a friend you are."

Bea chuckled. Francine put her hand on Lizzy's. "Tell me what interests you about Daniel."

"He's so incredibly gentle. He's huge, goodness, the man's as big as a house. In fact, he has to duck down before entering a room. Well, some rooms. But still, in spite of his size, I've watched him be so tender with the children. It's absolutely amazing. And I can't believe how fast he's learning what I teach him. He's a man of character, and yet he's so mysterious. For example, those scars on his wrists, how'd he get them? He said he was put in chains a time or two, but he never elaborates."

"The scars on his wrists are nothing compared to his back," Bea murmured. "He's had a very hard life, I'm afraid."

"His back?" Francine and Lizzy echoed.

"Yes, I saw a glimpse of it once when I went to the dock to speak with Ellis one day. Mo had his shirt off, just coming in from harvesting. . . I could see he'd been whipped and whipped often. Deep dark lines crisscross his back. It's a horrible sight." Bea's body shook from the memory.

"I never knew," Lizzy mumbled. A tear for Daniel and the pain he'd suffered under the hand of slavery burned a solitary path down her cheek.

" 'Tis no justice for what's been taken from a man, but we can thank the good Lord he's free now." Francine grasped her daughter's hand tighter. "Lizzy, if you love him, marry him. He'll come around."

"Personally, I don't see Mo offering marriage just to protect you. I can't imagine he doesn't have feelings for you too," Bea offered.

"Really? He's never said or showed it."

"Oh? Didn't you say the man had the young'uns prepare a special meal for you?" Francine reminded her.

Bea giggled.

"What?" Lizzy asked.

"I was just thinking, wouldn't it be fun to be a fly on the wall if you decide to tell Mo yes." Bea moved closer, leaning into them. "And to be there the day he discovers his true feelings for you. The man will be busting at the seams."

"Do you really think I should take him up on his offer to marry?"

"Sure, if ya love him," her mother responded. "The kids seem to like him."

"Like. . .enraptured is more like it. You should have seen them tonight. All seven of them huddled around and on him in the chair, each taking a turn reading to him."

"Ahh, I see you've got it bad for him," Francine teased. "So, what did you see in his lips?"

❧

Mo raised the frying pan, waiting for a response. He heard another sniffle. "Who's in here? Speak up before I blast ye."

"Mr. Mo, don't shoot. It's me, Benjamin."

"Benjamin, what are ye doing here at this time of night?" Mo lowered the frying pan.

"I heard you talking. . .talking with Momma."

"What did ye hear, Boy?"

"I heard Mr. Sanchez was mean to Momma and made her cry."

Thankfully the child didn't understand exactly what Mr. Sanchez had done.

"I want to kill him, Mo. I want to kill him real bad. He made Momma so afraid she can't go back to work."

Mo cradled the boy in his arms. "I know, Son, I knows the feeling. Yer Momma is okay, though; he didn't hurt her."

"But it ain't right," Ben protested.

"No, it ain't. Neither is yer sneaking out in the middle of the night."

"I know. But I can sneak in before Momma hears me."

Mo brightened the lamp in the kitchen.

"I'm the man of the house now. Well, when Uncle George ain't there," the boy amended. "I need to protect my momma."

"I'll protect yer momma," Mo said firmly. "Ye can help by watching over the other children."

"I've heard her crying, Mr. Mo. It's been real hard for Ma since Daddy died."

"I'm sorry, Son." What else could he say? He knew it had to be hard on a widow with four children. She was fortunate to have family to help her. "Would ye like something to drink?"

Benjamin nodded yes.

Mo went to the cupboard and pulled out a lemon and some sugar.

"Mr. Mo, did you mean what you said when you asked my momma to marry you?"

He heard that? Another knot tightened Mo's already tense stomach. "Yes, but she turned me down."

"Why?"

"I guess 'cause marrying me ain't something she ever thought about." Mo fumbled through the drawer looking for the juicer.

"Why'd you ask her?"

"I thought if we was married she wouldn't be having no

more trouble from Mr. Sanchez."

Ben curled his lower lip and nibbled it. Mo stifled a grin. It was the same nervous habit he'd seen Lizzy do so many times.

"I still want to beat him up." Benjamin pounded the table with his fist.

"Son, yer old enough to know right from wrong. But are ye old enough to learn to trust God with vengeance?"

"Huh?"

"A man's a real man when he can take the garbage of this world and trust God to change it in the end. I'm not sayin' I don't want to hurt Mr. Sanchez myself, but as a Christian, I hafta trust God. Only God can git back at men like Mr. Sanchez."

"How can God get back at someone who doesn't know Him?"

"I's cain't say whether Mr. Sanchez knows God or not. And I cain't say I'd hold my fist back if I wuz to see him right this very minute. Which is why I'm home and not in front of his house. But I do know that when the time comes, ifin I've given my anger over to God, I'll be able not to harm the man."

"If you hit him, you'd knock him over."

Mo chuckled. "Yer probably right. But when a man's been given more strength, God asks him to be more careful with it."

"I don't get it, Mr. Mo. You was a slave. Don't you hate men like Mr. Sanchez?"

"No, not really. I suppose some days I do. But most days I don't. I hate the sin. I hate the things my master did to me and to others around me. But I learned somethin' watchin' people die at my feet day in and day out in war. Life is special. Everyone deserves it; just not everyone appreciates it."

"Huh?"

"It's like this, Ben. Remember when ye wuz tellin' William he had to get a job?"

Ben looked down at his feet. "Yes, Sir."

"Well, ye weren't doin' somethin' God would be proud of now, were ye?"

"No, Sir," he mumbled.

"But ye learned from your mistake. Ye haven't tried it again, have ye?"

"No." Ben's head darted up and caught Mo's gaze.

"I didn't think so. See, some men don't learn from their sins; they just keep doin' 'em again and again. Like my master, fer example. He used to whip me over and over again. He was so afraid of me he just keep whippin' me. In his mind, he thought it wuz keeping me submissive.

"But I didn't submit, at least not the ways he thought I did. A slave doesn't know where to go, where to run to. He knows he needs to, and I knew I needed to, in order to save my life. But I wuz afraid to run. Afraid to be caught and have my foot half chopped off, or worse. My master, he wuz a mean one.

"But in order for him to really own me, he had to own my soul. And I never gave him my soul. When he beat me, I just concentrated on God, on my freedom in heaven one day, and took the pain. My master couldn't touch my soul. He tried. He tried mighty hard to break me. But he couldn't."

"Are those marks on your back from the whippings?" Ben asked.

Mo had forgotten he hadn't put his shirt back on when he came in from bathing. "Yes. I'm sorry ye saw them."

"Do they hurt?"

"No, they're just like any other scar ye can git from scraping yer knee on the ground. The pain is temporary. The scar's permanent and so is the memory."

Mo finished squeezing the lemon for Ben's drink. He added some water and sugar and swirled it together, then handed the glass to the boy.

"Thanks. So what can we do about Mr. Sanchez?" Ben asked, taking a healthy sip.

"Nothin'."

"Nothing? I've got to do something," Ben protested.

"No, Son, ye don't. It's up to yer mother. I'll walk her to work. That should stop Mr. Sanchez."

"But Momma said no."

"True, but I don't give in that easily." Mo winked. "I want ye to promise me you'll let me handle Mr. Sanchez and your mom about this. She be real embarrassed if she knew ye knew."

Ben curled his lower lip again. "All right."

"Good. Now ye best finish that drink and get on home before yer mother has yer hide fer sneakin' out like this."

"Will ya tell her?"

"Not if I don't have to."

"Thanks, Mo. And thanks for being a friend. Momma shoulda taken you up on your marriage offer, but I think I know why she didn't."

"Oh?"

❧

"Lips. I can't believe I let that slip, Lord." The heat of embarrassment still lingered on her face, while she tried to brush away the teasing thought that perhaps she should take Daniel up on his offer. *He does have a home with plenty of room.* She and the children would be very comfortable there, and he was the kind of man a woman could fall in love with.

Bea's comments about the scars on his back made her pause. How much did she really know about Daniel? And was it enough to marry him?

No, they were strangers, friends who had talked a few times, barely sharing their innermost thoughts. He'd shared very little about his life, and yet on a couple of occasions she had shared her heart.

Bea's words upon their parting tonight rang once again in her ears: "Perhaps the scars on his back reach all the way to his heart and he's afraid to open himself up."

"Lord, does Daniel have deep scars on his heart?" *Of course he does. He was a slave*, she chided herself, but then she shook her head. *You're making a mighty assumption here. Why must everyone who was a slave have deep heartaches?*

"You know, Jesus, I can't picture it any other way. I can't imagine a person being owned by someone and treated like nothing more than a cow or a chicken, not having anger and bitterness. Isn't that why Ben went off to fight? To free them? To stop the injustice of it all?" She'd read Frederick Douglass's *My Bondage and My Freedom* several times. Anger and bile rose in the pit of her stomach as she'd read the accounts of how he'd been raised as a slave. She could barely imagine what it would be like to be taken from your mother, near birth, and to have family members who meant nothing to you because you were never around them, or to be property, fit to be sold at the whims of a master. "Yes, that's why Ben went off to fight, Lord, and gave his life to free men and women locked in such bondage."

Lizzy passed the street toward Daniel's home and hesitated. Should she go tell him she'd be accepting his proposal? No, she wasn't settled on that. In some strange way, though, his proposal made sense. It seemed like the answer to her problems and prayers. And Daniel was right: If he were her husband he wouldn't be arrested for protecting his wife. But would she need to work? Could Daniel provide enough for her and her four children?

Her head throbbed. "Lord, I'm so confused."

Lizzy looked up at the stars and saw order in the heavens. She sighed. "Lord, put order back into my life, please."

twelve

Lizzy groaned as the children asked for their breakfast. "In a minute," she muttered, pulling the pillow up over her head. What a night. She'd hardly slept. And when she finally had fallen asleep—sometime around three, she guessed—she tossed and turned.

"Maaa," Sarah whined. "I'm hungry."

Where were those sweet little angels who had made dinner for her last night?

"Did Ben get the eggs?"

"He's still sleeping," Sarah pouted.

Ben sleeping? That wasn't like him. Lizzy threw off the covers and headed straight for Benjamin's room. His cherub face smiled in his sleep. *At least someone's content in this house,* she mused. She brushed her fingers across his cheek. His temperature was normal, his coloring fine. *He's just tired, I guess.*

The other six were in various stages of dress—some in their sleep wear, some in their underwear, and Vanessa, as always, was up and dressed with her nose in a book. "That girl sure loves to read, Lord," Lizzy muttered.

"George, would you go collect the eggs this morning?"

"Why can't Ben do it?" he whined.

Lizzy put her hands to her face and rubbed it, raking her fingers through her hair. She didn't need whiny children, not today. "George!" she snapped, raising her voice. The boy ran out the door without another question asked. The rest of the children stood at attention. Even Vanessa pulled herself away from the book. "Get dressed all of you. Vanessa, start cooking some oatmeal or cornmeal, which ever you prefer."

Lizzy headed into her room and freshened herself for the morning. It would be nice to have a day with no children, to get away like George and Clarissa. George and Clarissa would watch the children; they owed her that much for the times she watched theirs. But who would she go with?

An image of Daniel popped in her head. The thought of his rich mahogany eyes, black coffee hair, and deep walnut skin made Lizzy sigh. "You're right, Mother. I have got it bad."

How can a woman fall so deeply for a man who doesn't have the slightest romantic desires for her? "I'm in a sad state, Lord."

Dressed, hair in place, she went to the kitchen where George put down a basket of fresh eggs. "Thank you, George."

"You're welcome, Aunt Lizzy." He lowered his voice and leaned toward her. "Are you feeling better today?"

"Yes." She placed a hand on his shoulder. "Thanks for asking."

He nodded and headed for his room.

A knock at the front door made Vanessa holler, "I'll get it."

Lizzy dried off her hands and went to see who was there. "Morning, Mabel. Did you sleep well?"

"Yes, thanks. I'm here to watch the children so you can go to work."

Oh dear, in all her running around she hadn't told Mabel. . . "I'm sorry, I'm not going to work this morning."

"Is anyone sick?"

"No. Something came up."

Mabel looked puzzled, but she nodded and smiled. "Well, it's a fine day to not go to work."

"Thank you," Lizzy silently mouthed.

"So, what's burning in the kitchen?"

"Oh no." Lizzy went running back. The frying pan with the eggs was on fire. She pulled out a lid and plopped it on the frying pan. "Great, just great," Lizzy hissed.

"Lizzy, why don't I finish fixin' breakfast for the children? You go visit your mother or spend some quiet time at the beach."

"Are you sure?" Lizzy prayed Mabel wouldn't back down on her offer.

"Yes, I was planning on watching them. So take advantage of your day off." Mabel winked.

The children all watched with interest. They knew their mother wasn't completely back to her old self yet. "I think I'll take you up on your kind offer then."

"Wonderful. Be gone, Child. I can handle it from here."

Lizzy grabbed her purse, said good-bye to her children, except for the still-sleeping Ben, and headed out the door. She hadn't gotten far when she spotted Daniel.

"Lizzy, if ye insist on goin' to work, I'm walkin' ye."

She sucked in a deep breath and grabbed her courage with both hands. "Daniel, I'm happy to see you. We need to talk."

His dark coffee eyebrows raised.

"I've been thinking about your proposal."

"I'm sorry, I didn't mean to offend ye by it. I just figured it might be a good answer to yer problem. I knows I'm not much of a man to be marryin'. . ."

"Daniel Greene, I don't ever want to hear another word like that coming from my husband's mouth. You're a wonderful man, and any woman would be proud to have you as a husband."

His mouth hung open.

"Yes, you heard me right. I'm planning on marrying you. Now, when would you like to do this?"

❧

"Lizzy, are ye sure?" Daniel couldn't believe his ears. She was going to marry him, but why? Benjamin had made it perfectly clear that a woman like his mother wanted romance. And he just wasn't the romantic type.

"Yes. I thought about it long and hard last night. If you're willing to take on a wife with four children, I'd be a fool not to accept your generous offer."

Mo rubbed his face and then moved his hand to the back of his neck. He didn't remember being this nervous when he'd proposed marriage to Caron. "I'm willin'. I can provide fer ye and the children. I wouldn't want ye to go back to work."

"Are you sure?"

"I make good pay workin' fer Mr. Ellis. Yes, I can provide."

"If you don't want me to work, I won't work."

Lizzy looped her arm around his elbow. It felt wonderful to be so close to her. Could he keep his promise to have a marriage in name only? The heavenly scent of vanilla and. . . and. . . Mo sniffed. "Did you burn something this mornin'?"

"Uh, yeah." She looked toward the ground. "I normally don't burn the eggs."

Daniel chuckled. "Lizzy, I knows ye can cook. So, why'd ye burn the eggs?"

"Just that kind of a morning, I guess." She shifted her weight and looked up. Her hazel eyes, even more green today, shimmered in the sunlight. "Daniel, when do you want to get married?"

Today, he thought. "Are ye sure, Lizzy? Absolutely sure?"

"Yes. Oh, I know we don't know each other very well, but I think we can make a good marriage, Daniel. I'm not fooling myself. I know there's no romance between us. But you're a good man, and I'd be honored to have a man like you as my husband."

"Really?" He couldn't believe his ears. Here she was praising him again. Didn't she know he had been found unworthy by Caron? No, she didn't know anything about Caron, or anything about his life on the plantation.

"Yes. Are you having second thoughts, Daniel?"

He could feel her tremble against his arm. "No. Why don't we do it right now?"

"Now? Don't you want a wedding party?"

"I'm not one for crowds. I like small quiet things."

Lizzy giggled. "Then you'd better reconsider. Because with my family, nothing will ever be small."

He couldn't see himself rejoicing with a bunch of people about getting married with Lizzy. Not under these circumstances. If they had fallen in love. . . If they had gotten together like most men and women did. . .then perhaps a large party would be in order. How could he make her understand? He knew it had to be embarrassing to marry him like this. Benjamin told him his father had brought his mother flowers often. He'd give her frequent kisses. *Kisses*. He wasn't sure she'd accept a kiss from him. The idea of kissing Lizzy stirred a desire so deep he feared it. No, this was a marriage of convenience. But maybe in time. . . "Lizzy, I think we should get married right away, today in fact. Then plan a party for sometime in the future."

He wouldn't trust Mr. Sanchez for one moment, knowing his intentions toward her. No, the sooner they got married the better.

"All right, if that's what you'd like, Daniel."

"I think it best, Lizzy. Later we can celebrate. Now we need to make ye safe."

She stiffened in his arms.

"Let's go tell Mr. Sanchez ye won't be workin' fer them no more."

"I don't know if I can face him."

"That's all right. I'm yer husband; I can face him. Come on, Lizzy, show me which house is theirs."

He could feel her fear as she slowed her pace the closer they got to the house. "Ye stay here, Lizzy." He left her at the curb. "I'll be just a moment."

He pounded on the door. A Hispanic gentleman with black hair and a thin mustache opened the door. "May I help you?"

Daniel smiled. "Are ye Mr. Sanchez?"

"Yes. What can I do for you?"

"I'm Lizzy's husband."

The man instantly paled. "I've come to let ye know she won't be working fer ye no more." Daniel lowered his voice and leaned over the man. "And I don't ever want to hear that ye even looked at my wife again."

"Manuel, who's at the door?"

"Lizzy's husband; she's not going to be working for us any longer." Then he spoke Spanish to his wife, and Mo simply left him. It didn't matter what he told his wife. Mo knew he'd never lay a hand on Lizzy.

"What did he say?" Lizzy asked.

"Not a word, Dear. His tanned complexion paled to the color of buttermilk." Daniel winked.

"Thank you, Daniel. I just didn't know how to confront him."

"I'm certain he won't be botherin' ye again."

Daniel paused in the street facing town. "Since we're so close to the church, let's go see the pastor. I don't have a ring fer ye, Lizzy, but I'll get ye one."

"You don't have to."

"I want to. When the time is right, I'll get one. Right now, let's go make ye my wife and not make a liar out of myself. I introduced myself to Mr. Sanchez as yer husband."

"We wouldn't want to make you out to be a liar, now, would we?" She grinned.

"I'm afraid after the preacher marries us I have to go to work. I told Mr. Ellis I'd be late, but he's expectin' me by now. I'll be home a little late making up for lost time. I'll help ye move yer belongings over to my place in the evening."

❧

"You may kiss your bride." Daniel stiffened, and Lizzie winced. Was he afraid to kiss her?

He bent down and brushed her lips ever so gently. *Oh, Daniel, we've got so much to learn as a married couple.* They walked hand in hand down to the waterfront and to Mr. Ellis's dock.

"I'll be home around six, Lizzy."

"I'll be waiting." Lizzy headed on back to her house. She had to pack—and she needed help. She rushed to her mother's.

"You did what?" Francine planted her hands on her hips. "Goodness, Child, I suggested you get married, but I didn't think you'd go and do it the next morning."

"I know. I didn't know what to say to Daniel. He wanted to

get married right away. I was afraid if I said I wanted to wait a week or two until we could make a dress, plan a party, or something, that he'd think I didn't want him. Mom, he doesn't believe he's worthy of a wife."

"You've got your work cut out for you. But I'll come help you pack."

"Thanks, Mom. I'll see you at the house. I have to tell the children. I hope they understand."

Francine tossed her head from side to side. "You'll make them understand. It might take some time, but they'll get there."

"I'm most concerned with Benjamin. He remembers his father more than the others."

"Ben's a good boy. He'll come around."

"I hope you're right."

"I know I am. He comes from good stock." She winked.

Bea walked into the kitchen. "Did I hear right—you married Mo this morning?"

thirteen

"Foolish, huh?" Lizzy worked the linen napkin in her hands.

"Not necessarily, if you love him," Bea countered.

"Oh, I do. I don't love him like I loved Ben, but I do care for him."

"What's done is done. We should get to it, Child," her mother intoned. "Packing for five will take some doin'. Would you mind, Bea, ifin I help my daughter?"

"Of course not, as long as I get to help too. I'll bring Richie along to help as well."

"Help what?" Richie bounced into the room, his golden curls bouncing along with him.

"Help Miss Lizzy move her stuff to her new home."

"All right! Does that mean I can play with Henry and William today?"

Bea chuckled. "Yes, Dear."

"Thanks, Nanna! I'll go put on my play clothes."

Lizzy giggled. "He's still so cute. What are you ever going to do when this little one comes along?"

"Count on him being the big brother. He's become quite a little man around the house."

Richie shouted from down the hall, "Can I bring my checkers?"

"Sure." She turned back to the other two women. "Well, I better change into a dress I can work in as well. Richie and I will join you at your place as soon as possible. I'll hitch up the horse to the wagon. That'll make things go faster."

"Thank you, Bea. I really appreciate your willingness to help."

"Come on, Lizzy, let's get a move on. The day is slipping

away." Francine took her apron off and draped it on the kitchen chair.

Lizzy dropped the linen napkin she'd been wringing in her hands. She was more nervous than she thought. Following her mother out the door, she asked, "How should I tell the children?"

"Straight out. Ain't nothin' they can do about it now."

"Do you think they'll be upset?"

"Not if you put it in a positive light. For example, if you tell them they'll be getting new rooms and moving in with Mo, they might get all excited before they realize what it means that you've gone off and married him."

"Do you think I should have waited?"

"Yes. But God will work it out. It's as I told you last night, you both have feelings for the other—ye just haven't opened up and talked with each other about 'em."

"I do believe he'll be a good husband and father to the children."

"That's what counts. Honey, look. You're a grown woman. You know what it means to be married, and by them bags under your eyes, I'd say you didn't sleep much last night thinking about this."

"True."

"So, if you believe it's the right thing for you and Daniel to get married, then I'll respect your decision. Actually, I don't doubt the marriage part, just the timing. As a mother, I guess, I think you should have waited a few months, talked about your feelings, then decided. But. . ."

"But it's done now," Lizzy said with a smile.

"Yeah. Honey, I love you, and I'll support you in any way I can. You know that."

"Would you spend the night with the children? George and Clarissa are due back this evening but. . ."

"No need to explain. A wedding night should be private."

"Thanks, Mom. It's as you say—Daniel and I have a lot to talk about."

"Hmm, I was thinking about something other than talking. . . But you're right, the children don't need to be interrupting your private conversations tonight."

Oh dear, sharing Daniel's bed. . . Lizzy started to tremble.

"What's the matter?" Francine halted in the road.

"I just realized about, about. . ."

Francine swung her head back and roared with laughter. "You've been a widow too long. Come on, Child. We've got a marriage bed to make up as well as getting your belongings over to Mo's."

A marriage bed. Yes, she could make up the marriage bed, arrange the room, and even fix an intimate dinner for two tonight. It could be her wedding gift to her husband.

Husband. Daniel Greene was her husband. *Oh, Lord, help me be a good wife for him.*

❧

Ellis rubbed his beard. "You married her, just like that?"

"Yeah." Mo beamed.

"Goodness, Man, don't you know a woman likes to be wooed?"

"I guess I don't." Mo slumped his shoulders. "Have I done it all wrong?"

Ellis chuckled and slapped a hand on his back. "Mo, if she married you, just like that, I'd say she cares for you. And that's all that matters."

Should he tell Ellis that the marriage was really for her protection? That they were man and wife in name only? On the other hand, being married to Lizzy and keeping his end of the bargain of remaining "in name only" was going to be the most difficult test he'd ever encountered in his life. Even the whippings he'd endured as a slave would be nothing to living day and night beside that wonderful lady and not holding her, kissing her.

Oh, that kiss. . . Her lips were so soft.

"Mo, are you all right?" Ellis asked.

"I'm fine. I'm just realizing what I done."

Ellis roared with laughter. "Trust me, Mo, there's far more reality coming in the next few weeks. But, let me tell you, being married to a special woman is well worth anything you lose as a single man. In fact, there really isn't anything I miss about being single."

"That part ain't a problem. I didn't go out much anyway."

"Then what's the matter?"

"I—I'd rather not say."

"Fair enough. So, did you buy her a ring? Or get her a wedding gift?"

"No. Was I suppose to git her a gift?"

"You don't have to, but it's a nice gesture. I bought Bea a pearl necklace. She gave me this pocket knife." He pulled a knife out of his trousers. "Bea knew I was always looking for one, so she bought it. She had it engraved too."

"I wouldn't know what to git Lizzy. Pearls would look mighty purty on her."

"Yes, Lizzy's a fine looking woman."

"She takes my breath away sometimes."

"Glad to hear it. A man ought to feel that way about his wife. Well, come on, we've got some work to do. Why don't you leave early and fetch something from Peg Martin's store before you go home?"

Mo had been to the store a couple of times. Peg had some fine lace and linen table things. Would that make a good wedding gift for Lizzy? Jewelry sounded better, but he'd need to buy the wedding ring before he could buy her a necklace. Yes, he could provide for her and her children, but he'd have to be careful with his expenses. Very careful.

The day lingered on. Washing the sponges was boring, but at least here he didn't mess up the paperwork. Initially, Ellis had him working on the ledgers. After Mo's third mistake, Ellis sent him to work on washing the sponges. "I can see your mind is on other things today," Ellis had said with an understanding laugh.

Mo pushed the dry sponges down into the vat. Once they

soaked up the fresh water, he leaned his weight on them to squeeze out the water, then released them to fill up again. The monotonous job gave him time to think. *What can I get Lizzy for a wedding present?*

He pushed the sponges down into the vat again. A sharp pain ripped across his palm. When he pulled his left hand out of the vat, he found it covered with blood. "What on earth?" He looked down in the vat. His hand stung. "Mr. Ellis!" he hollered.

Ellis Southard came running out of the storeroom. "What's the matter. . .?" His gaze was fixed on Mo's hand. "What happened?"

"I don't know. I wuz cleanin' the sponges and somethin' sharp cut open my hand."

Ellis reached for his hand. "Let me look at it." Carefully, he looked over the wound. "There's too much blood. We need to wash your hand, and I think you're going to need stitches."

Mo sat down on the edge of the vat. Carefully, he fingered through the sponges until he found the sharp object. He fished it out and discovered a sponge had grown around a rusty knife. Using his knees to hold the sponge, he ripped it open with his good hand and pulled out the blade.

"Where did that come from?" Ellis asked, carrying a jug of water.

"Inside this here sponge. The thing just grew around it."

"Wonderful." Ellis shook his head. "Here, hold out your left hand so I can pour some water on it. With all that rust, we're going to need to flush this wound real good."

Mo gritted his teeth. The pain was intense, but he'd experienced worse. He knew about treating wounds, though he'd never had one from a rusty knife before. He'd known some men to die from getting cut with rusty objects. Even from stepping on a rusty nail. A cold shiver slid up his spine. He couldn't die, not when he'd just gotten married. What would happen to Lizzy?

❧

Ben grinned. "You married Mr. Mo?"

"Yes." What was going on in this boy's head? She had been certain he'd have the most trouble with the idea of her marrying Daniel, since he had the best memory of his father. Instead, he looked downright pleased.

"Good. When do we move into his house?"

Lizzy scratched her head. She wanted to clean out her ears. She couldn't possibly be hearing right. "Uhh, Grandma and I are here to start packing our stuff."

"I'll get George to help me pack mine and William's things." Ben turned around, his shoulders squared, and left to find the others.

Francine chuckled. "Not what you expected."

"Not in the least. Something isn't right."

"Maybe you're not giving the boy enough credit. He's getting to that age where he thinks he's all grown up."

"Yeah, I know."

"Could also be the young'uns took a shine to Mo."

"Apparently. Mom, he didn't even flinch. He just took the information as a matter of fact. I'm not ready for this." Lizzy snickered.

"No parent is. We just do the best we can and pray we survive it. This is the good part, the confident part. Then comes the I-don't-have-a-clue-but-I'm-not-listening-to-you part. Them days are hard. You were the toughest of my children."

Lizzy wanted to protest. She'd seen George give their mother a lot more grief during his teen years than she ever did. Her memory was that she had been their easy child. But then again, her memory was biased. *Guess I'll be asking Mom more questions in the days to come,* she mused.

"Let's get packing. Bea should be here pretty soon." Francine rolled up her sleeves and headed for Lizzy's room.

"Wasn't it only a year ago we were doing the same for you, Mother?"

"Just about. A little over a year since I moved in with the Southards."

"Do you miss your own house?"

"Oh, maybe sometimes. But then I get to thinking about how many of you live here. I like my nice quiet room all to myself—and the fact that there's only one child under foot instead of seven."

Lizzy giggled. "Not for long." Lizzy reached under the bed and pulled out the crate where she kept her extra bed linens. Since moving into her mother's house, she'd been sleeping with her daughters in one double bed.

"True, but I can't imagine the Southards wanting seven children."

Bea walked into the room. "Oh, Cook, didn't we tell you, Ellis decided to have a dozen?"

"Dozen? You best have a talk with that man. Or is he planning on birthing half of them himself?" The room erupted with laughter.

Lizzy moved to the dresser and began to remove some of the girls' clothing.

"Where do you want me?" Bea asked.

Lizzy looked at the dresser drawers. "You know, this would probably be the best job for you since it's all got to go. I do want to leave an outfit for the girls to dress in tomorrow."

"Great, I can handle this." Bea stepped up to the dresser.

"I'm going to go to the kitchen and take some of my pots and pans. I wouldn't take them, but Mo has next to nothing in his kitchen."

"George and Clarissa will understand." Francine opened the closet. "Is everything in here yours?"

"I think so. I'm sure you'll be able to tell, Mom."

Francine nodded. Lizzy left and headed to the kitchen.

"Momma," Sarah whined, "Ben says you're married to Mr. Mo and that we'll be moving to his house."

Oh, dear. She knew she should have gathered them all together before she told one of them. Unfortunately, Ben had been the only one in the house. The rest had gone over to Mabel's but now they were back.

Lizzy sat in a chair. "Come here, Honey."

Sarah inched toward her with her lower lip puffed out.

"Here, sit on my lap." Lizzy patted her legs and her daughter plopped down. "The answer to your question is, yes."

"Why?"

Why indeed? The children had no understanding of the events that had transpired yesterday. Was it only yesterday? Lizzy could feel the weariness start to overtake her body. Her arms felt heavy and her eyelids felt worse. "It's hard to say in one word. But I like Mr. Mo, and he asked me."

"But don't people marry because they love each other?"

"Oh, I love Mr. Mo." It's just a different kind of love from what her daughter was picturing. She was old enough to see how George and Clarissa responded to each other. The kissing, the holding hands—none of these she'd seen her mother do with Daniel. She certainly could understand her daughter's confusion.

"Don't you like Daniel?"

"I like him, but I don't know about him being my daddy."

"Daniel will never replace your father. But I think he'll make a great second daddy, since yours went to heaven."

"Will I have my own bed, or will I have to share it with you and Mr. Mo? He's really big, and Olivia and I already take up a lot of room in the bed."

Lizzy stifled a chuckle. "No, Honey. You and Olivia will be sharing your own bed in your own room."

"Where you going to sleep, Momma?"

"With Daniel, in another room. Like Uncle George and Aunt Clarissa."

"Oh. Then it's okay if you marry Mr. Mo."

"Thank you, Dear." She wasn't about to point out to her daughter that the deed was already done. But it was nice to have two of her children's blessings. Now to hear from William and Olivia.

"Grandma is here with Mrs. Bea, packing in our room. Would you like to give them a hand?"

Sarah nodded and wiggled off her lap. Lizzy got up and started working her way through the cupboards. From what she could recall of James Earl's kitchen, she would need quite a few of her pots and pans. She did have a crate or two in the back shed with some of her belongings that had not been needed in her mother's house.

"Momma," called William, as he and Olivia scrambled into the kitchen with Mabel following close behind. "You married Mr. Mo?"

"Yup."

"Yipee!" William hooted.

Olivia popped her thumb in her mouth and sidled up beside her mother. Lizzy hadn't seen her suck her thumb in several months. "Liv, what's the matter?"

"Are you still going to be my momma?" Olivia mumbled around her thumb.

fourteen

"If you keep this clean, Mo, you shouldn't get lockjaw," Doc Hanson said, as he finished stitching up the injured hand and then wrapped the wound with white gauze. "Here, take this home with you and change the bandage tomorrow."

With his good hand, Mo reached out and took the rolled bundle of gauze. "Thank ye, Doc. What do I owes ye?"

"Nothing," Ellis chimed in. "You were injured working for me, so it's my responsibility to pay for your medical."

Ellis forked over a couple of bills to the doctor. Mo fought with his pride, but he was grateful that Ellis was paying. He wouldn't have gone to the doctor if it hadn't been for Ellis, though he was glad he had after he saw the doctor fish out bits of shell and sand from deep inside the wound. Not many doctors recognized the need to make sure wounds were cleansed well.

Mo was relieved. Facing the possibility of death on his wedding day didn't set well with him. Although the idea of not being able to work for a week right after he'd taken on the expenses of a wife and four children made him concerned in a whole new way.

The hand bandaged and the doctor paid, he and Ellis left the doctor's office and headed back toward the dock. "Don't know what you can do for me with that hand, Mo."

"I know, Sa. I'd be willin' to work one-handed."

"No, you heard what the doc said about infection. You'll need to keep it clean, Mo. And this job is anything but a clean job."

"I know." A week without pay. He had some savings, but that was for a rainy day. And what about buying Lizzy a wedding gift? This day sure had been an expensive one. First a couple bucks to the preacher for the wedding, now the loss of work, and the wedding gift. Could he really afford a gift at this time? On the other hand, his rainy-day fund hadn't been dipped into, except for James's funeral.

Ellis reached into his pocket and pulled out his wallet. "Here, Mo." He handed him some bills. "This is your pay for the week."

"But I's didn't work fer it."

"True, but like I said in the doctor's office, you were injured on the job. I don't want to lose you. If you were one of my other divers, I might only give him a couple of days' pay. But with you, well, you deserve it. Some of the others we can't count on. You've seen that."

"Yes, Sa." Mo covered the bills in his hand, clenching his fist, then shoved them into his pocket. He looked around the area to see if anyone had seen him putting away the money. He wasn't about to get his head banged again. The sheriff had a suspect and he was keeping an eye on him, but the sheriff couldn't prove anything yet. The fellow had some money that same day and had gotten himself rather drunk that evening, but that was circumstantial evidence.

"Also, when you have time to count the money, you'll find your pay is doubled," Ellis went on. "Since you're doing so well with the reading and writing, I'm hiring you on as my foreman."

"But I still don't understand yer books," Mo protested, reaching back into his pocket to give back some of the money.

"Tomorrow I want you to come to work and take the ledger home with you. See if Lizzy can understand them, and see if she can help you understand them better than I."

Mo nodded. He certainly did learn faster with Lizzy as his teacher. No offense to Mr. Ellis, but he sure did make things confusing.

Ellis chuckled. "Your face reveals a lot, Mo. I can see you agree Lizzy might be a better teacher."

Mo grinned. "Well. . ."

The two were still laughing when they stepped into Southern Treasures. "Morning, Peg," Ellis said as he entered.

"Morning, Ellis, Mo. What can I do for you?"

"Good morning, Miz Martin. I'm wondering if ye might have some of that fancy lace work ye do?"

Peg Martin's fair face beamed. "Sure do. It's over to the right."

"Thank ye." Mo headed toward the area she pointed out. He had in mind to get Lizzy a linen tablecloth with a lace border. But his eyes caught a cloth with embroidered flowers.

"Mo, I'll see you tomorrow." Ellis waved and headed out the door.

"Ellis tells me you went and got yourself married, Mo."

"Yes'm. Lizzy Hunte."

"Congratulations. Lizzy's a fine woman."

"Thank ye."

"Can I help you?" Peg stepped closer to him. For a single woman, she'd always seemed very sure of herself. And she was one of the few folks who hadn't been intimidated by his size the first time she met him.

"I want to give Lizzy a special gift. I have a couple pearls I've collected from some oysters, but I knows it would cost too much for me to have 'em put in some purty setting."

"Wish I could help you, Mo. But my handcrafting is limited to embroidery and such."

He had figured as much. "I like this cloth, here. What kind of flowers are these?" The bright purple flowers with a tiny center of yellow seemed to be salt and peppered around the border of the cloth.

"Those are African violets."

"I like the deep purple." And he'd love to see Lizzy in a dress made from the same rich color.

"I have matching napkins that go with that cloth. You're in luck—I just finished the last one this morning, shortly before you came in."

Tablecloth and napkins. Could he afford both? His countenance brightened as he remembered his pay had just doubled. "How many napkins?"

"A set of eight. Should be enough for you, Lizzy, and the four children."

"Thanks, I think I'll buy them."

"Wonderful. Can I wrap it up for you?"

Mo wondered if wrapping a gift was necessary.

"I received this beautiful paper in the other day, and I'd love to dress this gift up for your bride. No charge, Mo. It'll be my wedding gift to you."

"Thank ye. I think Lizzy would like a fancy wrapped present."

Peg pushed her blond hair behind her shoulders. "As a woman, I know she will."

Ahh, that was the problem. As a man he didn't know what a woman liked. Yes, Peg Martin would be quite helpful in the decisions he'd make in terms of gifts.

Peg bent and picked up the tablecloth and brought it over to the counter. "You know, Mo, if you have some pearls you want put in a setting you might want to talk with the jeweler."

"I don't think I can afford that right now."

"Oh, I understand. On the other hand, you might want to talk with him anyway. He might be willing to buy those pearls."

"Not sure I trust the man—don't know him."

Peg knitted her eyebrows and glanced up at him. Then a realization crossed her face. "If you trust me, I'd be happy to ask him what the value of the pearls are. Personally, I've never done business with the man, but I haven't heard folks complaining about him either."

Mo scratched his chin with his good hand. His left hand was beginning to throb. "I might take ye up on that. I need to get Lizzy a weddin' ring. Maybe he'll barter for some pearls."

"Might be a good idea. So, where'd you get these pearls?"

"I've been collecting some oysters when I'm harvesting the

sponges. Since I've been working for Mr. Ellis, I've found three."

"Wow, maybe I should start oystering." Peg smiled and continued to place the tablecloth and napkins in the fancy paper.

"I found a rose-colored one and two white ones."

"Rose one would be worth more." She folded the paper over the bundle and held it together with a thin string. Then she grabbed a pale pink ribbon woven into a ribbon of lace.

"Yer making this look mighty purty. Thank ye, Miz Peg."

"You're welcome. Would you like me to go with you to the jeweler's now?"

"I don't have the pearls on me. I keep 'em in a safe place."

"Wise. I heard you had a run-in awhile back."

Mo rubbed the back of his head. "Afraid so."

"So what say you, yes or no to my accompanying you to the jewelers?"

"All right. Can we leave Lizzy's gift here? I wouldn't want to soil it."

"Sure." Peg escorted him out of the shop, pulled a key she had hid around her neck, and locked the store. "So, when did you and Lizzy start having feelings for one another?"

❧

Lizzy stood in Daniel's kitchen, wondering where she should begin. Her head was pounding. The lack of sleep and the long morning of packing and unpacking had left her even more exhausted. Ben should be here shortly, she hoped. She'd sent him to the docks to see if he could buy some fresh fish or lobster for the special dinner she planned for Daniel tonight. It was the least she could do. "But what besides fish can I feed the man?" she mumbled.

Again she opened the cupboard that contained a few food items. Some dry beans, rice, flour, and some brown sugar. He had a few spices, but nothing compared to her cupboard back at her house.

"This is your house, Lizzy old girl, you best get used to it." She amused herself, speaking like her mother. Her mother and Bea had left about a half hour earlier. "Mangoes. That's it! I'll get some fresh mangoes from the Southard's tree."

She removed her apron, straightened her dress, and headed out the door as Bea drove up with her carriage. "Bea, what on earth are you doing back here?"

"Cook and I decided you needed some basics for the kitchen. Have you had a look at that man's shelves?"

Lizzy giggled. "Yeah, I was coming to your place to get some fresh mangoes. I'm hoping Ben can come back with some fresh fish or lobster."

"Sounds delicious. Well," Bea reached over and pulled a box from the seat next to her. "I've got some mangoes here, some limes, and a couple of canned vegetables your mother and I put up."

"Thank you."

"I also put in some dried herbs that I grew this winter." Bea handed the box over. "You know, I'm still not used to saying that. Up North you can't plant anything in the winter. And yet, down here, it's better for a lot of the crops to be planted and harvested in the winter months."

Lizzy smiled. "For me, the idea of only being able to plant four months out of the year sounds really strange."

"I guess it's all a matter of perspective, huh?" Bea got down from the wagon. "I also had a set of dishes that I was given as a wedding present. I've never used them. Ellis had such a full house before I married him. Anyway, I figured you could make better use of them than just sitting in my closet."

"I can't take your wedding present."

"Sure you can. It's from a distant cousin who will never come down here. And even if Grettel does come, I know she won't be offended."

Bea started to lift the box of dishes. "Let me get that. You carry this one," Lizzy offered.

Bea pondered the idea for a moment then, looking at her blossoming tummy, readily agreed. "I keep forgetting."

"Soon there'll be no forgetting."

"So I hear."

Ben came running up. "Mom, Mr. Mo had an accident."

Lizzy felt her knees go weak. "What happened?"

"Mr. Ellis said he was washing the sponges and one of them had a knife inside it."

"What?"

"A rusty old knife. The sponge just grew around it." Ben leaned over and placed his hands on his knees while he caught his breath.

"Mercy, is he all right?"

"Mr. Ellis says his hand is cut up, but he should be okay."

"Where is he?"

"Don't know. He wasn't working for Mr. Ellis when I got there. He said Mr. Mo can't work for a week, or until his hand heals."

Oh dear, no work for a week. Can Mo afford that and us? "What should I do?"

"Not a thing. Wait for him to come home and he'll tell you all about it. Then you two can decide what to do. Obviously, he went to Doc Hansen," Bea said confidently, placing a loving hand on her shoulder.

"Yup, Mr. Ellis went with him. Said he was stitched up with fifteen stitches."

Didn't the man have enough scars on his body already? *Lord, what's happening here?*

"Come on, Lizzy, let's get these things settled in the kitchen." Bea turned to Ben. "What did you get from the fisherman?"

"Oh, a couple of lobsters."

"Great." Bea headed into the house, and Ben trailed after her. Lizzy stared at the crate of dishes wrapped with straw and brown paper. She thought of Daniel, the cut on his hand, rusty nails, and the loss of her young brother some twenty years ago because he had stepped on a nail. A shiver slithered down her spine, "No, Lord, please. . . No."

fifteen

"Thank ye." Mo extended his hand to Nathaniel Farris, the owner of the jewelry store.

Nathaniel grasped his hand firmly and shook it. "Pleasure doing business with you, Mo."

Peg Martin, having come in with him, no doubt helped with the warm reception he'd gotten from Mr. Farris. "Thanks, Peg."

"Pleasure, Mo. Now take that ring home to your pretty new wife, and I'm sure Mr. Farris will be happy to see you in the morning." Peg smiled.

"I appreciate this, Mr. Farris."

"Well, as I said earlier, if you have a pink pearl it will more than cover the cost of the ring. But if it's not of the right value, I'm sure the other two pearls will more than compensate."

"I've got to get back to my store, Mo." Peg stepped toward the door.

"I'll come with ye to pick up Lizzy's gift."

The jeweler handed Mo a small box, which he slipped into his pocket. Maybe this day wasn't going to be as expensive as he'd thought. Peg's fingers seemed a bit thicker than Lizzy's, so they had found a ring that was just a bit too tight for her. He hoped he wouldn't have to bring it back, but Mr. Farris said it wouldn't be a problem either way.

"Thanks, Miz Peg. I don't think he would have given me the ring today without yer say so."

"Ah, it's nothing. Happy to help."

Peg went to unlock the door to the store and stopped. "It's not locked, Mo. I swear I locked it."

"You did, I saw ye. Let me go in first."

Mo grabbed the doorknob and stepped inside the store. His

gift for Lizzy sat on the counter. He listened. Hearing nothing, he stepped deeper inside. A floorboard creaked, and it wasn't one under his foot.

"Call the sheriff, Miz Martin," Mo hollered, and blocked the front door.

A thin man with a scraggly beard stood up from behind the counter. He cocked a crooked smile. "Ain't took nothin'."

"Good, but ye can tell the sheriff, not me."

"I think I'll just be leavin' before the sheriff gets here." He stepped from behind the counter.

"I don't think so."

"Who's goin' to stop me, you?"

"Appears so." Mo inhaled deeply, crossing his arms in front of his chest.

"I knocked ya down before, big boy. I can do it again."

Then Mo saw a thick hickory club behind the man's back.

"Ye may have hit me once when I wasn't lookin' but today is a different day. And I don't make the same mistake twice." Mo knit his eyebrows and peered down at the dirty, disheveled man. The muscle of his jaw tightened. He opened and closed his hands in front of the man, letting him get a good inspection of his size and strength.

The thief pulled the stick from around his back and raised it shoulder length, holding it with both hands. "This here is none of your concern. Back off."

"Oh, I think this is my concern. Come on give me a chance to pay ye back for the clunk on my head," Mo dared the weak man.

Seeing Mo's determination, the man paled.

Mo dared him again. "Come on."

The man dropped the club to the floor.

"Wise man. I'm sure ye heard the stories about Samson in the Bible and his bein' able to kill a lion with his bare hands. Well, if you've been around here long, you'll have heard I did near the same one night when a black panther came after me."

The man fell to his knees and raised his hands. "Don't hurt me," he pleaded.

"Move aside, Mo. I'll take it from here." The sheriff came in and placed handcuffs on the sniffling man.

"Ye best tell the sheriff what you used that club for before," Mo advised.

The man cackled. "No proof. Why hang myself?"

Mo stared at him long and hard. "Sheriff, did ye hear the story about the panther?"

"Sure did. Ellis Southard told me." The sheriff winked. The fact was it was just a story. Something someone made up.

"And can ye believe this here fella doesn't want to tell ye he's the one that hit me over the head a couple months back? Amazing." Mo wagged his head back and forth to exaggerate his feigned astonishment and took a threatening step closer.

The man gave a whimper of fear. "Oh, all right. I knocked him out and took his silver pieces."

"Thought so," the sheriff said grimly. "I was just waiting for you to make your next move, Joe Everly. For future reference, after you get out of my jail you best move on. This island is small and folks around here know everything about everyone. You won't be getting away with your shenanigans around here." The sheriff pushed Mr. Joe Everly out the door. Then he turned back to Mo. "What I hear true about a new bride?"

"Yes, Sa." Mo grinned.

"Congratulations."

Peg's voice wavered next to him. "Thanks, Mo. I hate to think what would have happened to me if you weren't here."

❧

The lobster tails were prepared and ready for cooking; the rice and beans simmered in a pot. A fruit and nut salad with the mangoes, chopped almonds, and lime juice rounded out the meal. Lizzy wiped the sweat from her brow. She wondered what was keeping Daniel in town and fought the dark thoughts that something bad had happened to him.

She was exhausted. She needed a few minutes of sleep

before Daniel came home. But first she needed to freshen up. If Daniel should come home before she awoke, she didn't want him to see her in this state.

The china pitcher and basin on the commode provided welcome relief. Either Bea or her mother had filled it and placed small hand towels and wash rags in the drawer. Lizzy stripped and washed herself. She took from the closet a fresh cotton blouse with puffy short sleeves and a laced neckline. The next item was a long Spanish-style skirt that gathered at the waist, and seemed the perfect attire in which to greet her new husband.

Dressed, she slipped back into the kitchen, stirred the black beans, removed the rice from the heat, and placed it on the side of the stove where it would stay warm but not cook further. Lizzy didn't want the first meal she made as Mrs. Daniel Greene to be a disaster. She tossed the fruit salad, blending its juices, and glanced at the table.

She'd set it with the new dishes Bea had given her, and with some silverware she'd found in Daniel's kitchen. A small Mason jar was filled with bright red and pink hibiscus. Lizzy smiled. "Oh, Daniel, I hope you're pleased."

She scurried off to the bedroom and lay down on the bed. Soon he'd be home, and they needed to talk. Her eyes closed. Sleep overtook her weary body immediately.

❧

"Lizzy."

Someone was calling her. She rolled over and snuggled deeper into her pillow.

"Lizzy."

Daniel! She sprang from the bed, straightened her hair and clothing, then walked into the kitchen. He stood staring at the table.

"Hello, Daniel."

"Ye did all this?" He pointed to the table, then around to the stove.

"Yes. I wanted to make you a special dinner."

"Smells great." He looked down at his soiled clothing. "I'm not fit for such a feast."

She saw the bandage on his hand. "Ben said you were injured."

He held up his hand. "Yeah, a sponge grew around a knife. Doc said I should be all right."

Under his other arm she saw a fancy, wrapped package.

"Where's the children?" he asked.

"Home. I mean, home at their old home. My mother is watching them until George and Clarissa get settled in from their trip." She looked down at her bare toes. "I wanted to give us some privacy."

Daniel came up beside her. "Oh, Lizzy girl, ye didn't have to do that. But I'll cherish the night alone with ye. I suspect we won't have many of those until the young'uns are grown and married."

Lizzy smiled. "I suspect you're right."

"Here, I bought ye something. A weddin' gift."

"Oh, Daniel, you didn't have to do that."

"We had a rushed weddin'. Thar's a bunch of things we haven't done or discussed, but I've been told a man gives his wife a gift. So I went and got ye a little something. When I saw it, I thought of ye."

"May I open it now?"

"Yes."

Lizzy sat down on a chair at the table for two she'd fussed over earlier. She pulled the lace bow and it opened, revealing the hand-embroidered napkins. "They're beautiful."

"I think the purple is the perfect color for ye. Peg says they are African violets."

She placed the bundle at her place setting and jumped up into her husband's arms. She leaned up on her toes and threw her arms around his neck. "Bend down, Daniel. I can't kiss you."

Daniel bent down and she placed a gentle kiss on his lips. He scooped her up in his arms and held her tightly. "Lizzy, I know I said we would have this marriage be in name only. But. . ."

She cut him off. "Daniel Greene, I did not marry you and not expect to do my wifely duty. A marriage is a marriage, and I aim to make this as good of a marriage as I possibly can."

"Ye mean it?"

"Yes."

He brought her gently to the ground. "I'm glad. Cause after that kiss in front of the preacher I was thinkin'. . . Well, ye don't want to know what I was thinkin'."

Lizzy chuckled. "I think I can imagine."

"Let me clean up. I got dried blood on my pants. Then I have to tell ye about my day."

"Sure. I'll cook the lobster tails while you're changing."

Mo stepped into the bedroom. "Woman, how did ye get all of this done in just a few hours?" he called.

"I had help. My mother and Bea gave me a hand."

"Lizzy girl, yer amazing."

❧

Father, God, thank Ye for Lizzy. Thank Ye that she wants to make this a real marriage. Help me be the kind of husband she needs, Daniel silently prayed.

He glanced at the bed. It had fancy white pillowcases with embroidered flowers on them and a white spread over the mattress that spoke volumes of just how feminine this woman he married was. Could he possibly be sensitive enough for her?

"When I wuz at Southern Treasures I stopped a man from robbing it."

"What?"

Daniel scrubbed his chest and under his arms.

Lizzy came up behind him—and gasped when she saw his naked back.

Daniel turned. "I'm sorry."

"Sorry? What are you sorry for? Goodness, Daniel, who whipped you like that?"

"My master. He wuz a short and very insecure man. He

thought the best way to keep me in submission wuz to keep whippin' me."

Lizzy came up beside him and lightly touched the scars. He saw tears fill her eyes.

"Each stripe on my back made me more determined to leave the plantation, but I never had enough confidence that I could do it."

She traced a scar that ran diagonally across his back. He felt the warmth of her feather-like touch.

"How often did he beat you?"

"I don't know."

"I'm sorry you had to live that way, Daniel."

He put down the washcloth and lifted her to the bed. Then he knelt down beside her. "Lizzy, it's a horrible life, no question about it. In fact, youse almost don't even feel like yer alive. Ye have no say about what ye can do. You're treated like chattel. In fact, you're called that by yer white masters. But God's showed me that He goes to the darkest pit and gives His love to everyone."

She placed her hands in his and gently touched his fingers.

"I knows ye were born free, but was someone in yer family a slave?"

"Yes. I've heard stories. But I've never seen a man so badly beaten like you were."

"Thar's more, and someday I'll tell ye. But tonight is a night for celebratin'. If ye don't mind, I'd like to talk about my life as a slave another time. I'd rather concentrate on being a free man tonight, and on all the blessings God has given me."

Lizzy smiled. "You're right. There'll be plenty of days to talk about both our pasts. I'd like to tell you about Ben sometime. I think you would have liked him."

Daniel smiled. Ben was a part of her past, just as Caron and slavery were a part of his. Yes, he'd like to know about Ben, but not tonight. He already knew from Ben's son that they had had a happy marriage. How could he compete?

"So, what were you saying about Peg Martin's store?"

"Oh, well, I got yer gift from her store and we left the store for a bit. When we's came back the door had been unlocked, and so I went in. Thar wuz this man. . ." He told her the entire story.

"I'm glad the man who attacked you is behind bars. I hope he stays there. We don't need folks like that on Key West."

"Nope."

"But what's this about the panther and Samson?"

"A while back, before I came to ye fer lessons, someone tried to blame me fer some other trouble in town. Pretty soon a rumor wuz spread that I'd taken a black panther and killed it with my bare hands. Ain't true, but it has kept people from challengin' me to a fight every time I turn around. I've kinda adopted the story."

Lizzy chuckled. "Don't you think your size is enough?"

"It's because of my size that I'm always bein' challenged."

"I suppose. I never understood that about men."

"Me neither, just part of being a man, I guess."

The sound of water hissing as it hit the hot stove made Lizzy jump up from the bed. "I forgot the lobsters."

Mo got up off his knee and went to the closet. Inside, he found Lizzy's dresses hanging next to his trousers. He grinned. "Guess, I'm really married, Lord."

sixteen

Lizzy caressed Daniel's chest as she nuzzled in closer. "Good morning," she whispered. She caught a glimpse of the sparkling gold band on her hand. Daniel had given it to her last night. Moment by moment she was falling deeper in love with this man. Perhaps it wouldn't take too long before they really knew and understood each other.

"Mornin', Mrs. Greene." Her heart soared. He wrapped his arm around her. "What would ye like to do today?"

His bandaged hand came up and caressed her cheek. Her eyes caught a glimpse of the bloodstained bandage. She bolted up in bed. "Daniel, you were bleeding."

He lifted his palm to get a better glimpse of it. "I guess I wuz."

"Didn't the doctor say we needed to change the bandage?"

"Yes."

"Come on." Lizzy slid out of bed and pushed her hair behind her shoulders, then grabbed her robe hanging on the back of the door. "Where's the gauze that Dr. Hanson gave you?"

Daniel sat up in bed and lifted his knees, resting his elbows on them. "Uh, I don't know. Wait, let me think. My pants, in one of the pockets."

Lizzy grabbed the pitcher. "I'll fetch some fresh water and a pair of scissors. You can fetch the gauze."

A cock crowed in the distance. *The sun's up, so the birds must have overslept. Just like yourself, Lizzy, old girl.* It had been natural staying so long in bed, with Daniel not needing to go to work. They had talked and talked until the wee hours of the morning. A bond developed last night, a bond that would create the foundation for their marriage. *Forgive me, Ben. I may learn to love him with the same fiery passion I felt for you.* Lizzy jumped, startled at herself for thinking of Ben now. On the other hand, wouldn't it be natural? Ben was the only other man she'd ever loved.

She fished a pair of scissors from a kitchen drawer and pumped the water into the pitcher. Quickly she walked back to their bedroom. "Daniel, I've got the. . ." Her voice caught in her throat. The scars on his back reminded her of his past. Of the life he'd been forced to live. She swallowed down the raw emotions of anger and the bile of bitterness. This was what Ben fought for after all.

"Ye will get used to it." He turned and he reached for his shirt.

"I suppose, but it just makes me more determined."

"Determined to what?" he asked and sat down on the edge of the bed, holding out his injured hand.

"Oh, I don't know."

"Why don't we just keep working where God's put us? Thar young'uns here that need your teaching. If ye wasn't here to teach them, who would? We have to raise the children to become educated, to learn a trade, to make a life for themselves and their families." Daniel reached out and lifted her chin. "Lizzy, I don't run away from a fight, but this one is a big 'un, and we's need to do what we can where we can."

"I suppose you're right."

"I knows I am. At one point I'd thought of usin' this here house as a school fer Negroes and to set ye up as the teacher. We can still open the house, but with us married we'll also be needin' the rooms fer the children."

"You thought about setting up a school?"

"Yes'm. Ye taught me so much. I'm still learnin', but my eyes are open. I can see signs and know what they say. Or, at least, sound them out. Takes me a bit, but I'm gettin' thar." He locked his brilliant mahogany eyes with hers; their red hues sparkled with his fiery belief in education. "Ye have a very important role on Key West, Lizzy. Ye can read; ye can teach. God's given ye a gift."

Unable to speak, she lowered her glance to his injured hand. "Let me cut off this soiled bandage." He held out his hand. She snipped the edges and worked the bandage open, down the side of his hand. "Oh, my," she gasped. "How big was that knife?"

"Six-inch blade."

Blood had dried on the edges of the wound, though the gauze had soaked up most of it. "You can still move your fingers?"

Daniel demonstrated, lightly brushing her arm with his fingers.

Lizzy swallowed. "I guess so."

Daniel chuckled. "Yer a fine woman, Elizabeth Hunte Greene, and Caron pales in comparison to ye."

"Caron? Who's Caron?"

❧

Oh no, this wasn't how he'd planned to tell Lizzy about Caron. "She wuz the woman I wuz engaged to."

"What happened?" Lizzy's nimble fingers cleansed around the wound, her touch so gentle, the warmth of her breath so personal. *Goodness, Lord, she's beautiful.*

"I wuz twenty-two, and we wuz all set to get married, when my master discovered how set I wuz on her. That's when he. . ." Daniel coughed to clear his thickening throat. "When he bedded her."

"Oh, Daniel, how horrible. She must have died."

"No. The worst part of it wuz, she preferred what the master offered over me. That wuz why I ran. I had nothin' left at the plantation. And to see Caron day and night, and knowin'. . . Well a man can't live with himself under that kind of circumstance."

"I can understand that."

"It's not all Caron's fault. The best jobs, so's to speak, for a female slave wuz to be taken in like that. And she didn't know there wuz any life other than the life of the plantation. Which is no life at all. It's hard comin' from a plantation to livin' on yer own. Yer confused, lost, and alone. Some days ye even wonder ifin ye should go back."

He and Lizzy continued to talk about his days on the run, his time in the service of the Union Army, and the various changes he went through realizing what freedom meant to him. Even today he still worried that someone might snatch him and tell him the government had changed its mind about freeing the slaves.

"Hey, Mom, Mr. Mo, are you in here?" Benjamin called from the front door.

"Oh, goodness, I'm not dressed yet." Lizzy clutched her robe and got up off the bed where they had been talking.

"Ye got yer night gown and robe on. Hasn't yer young'uns seen ye in that before?"

"Yes, but. . .well it's so late in the day." A dusky pink rose on her delicate cheeks.

"I'm in my room," Lizzy called out.

Her room. Mo certainly did enjoy hearing that.

Ben stood at the doorway. "Oh, what a cut." Benjamin's brown eyes rounded to the size of saucers.

Mo looked down at his hand. The knife had cut clear across his palm.

"Does it hurt?" Ben asked.

"Some, not too much. Son, yer mother and I needs to dress. Would ye excuse us?"

"Sure, the others will be here shortly. I ran ahead." Ben puffed up his chest.

"Why don't ye go help Olivia? Her little legs must be tired by now."

Ben nodded, and Mo closed the door. Lizzy hastily bandaged his hand.

"You handled him like an experienced father. I'm proud of you." Lizzy draped her arms around his neck.

"Didn't ye say yer mother was watchin' 'em last night?"

"Yes. Depending on when George and Clarissa got home, she might have stayed the night."

Mo lifted her off the floor and held her close to his chest. "Then I suggest ye get dressed," he said with a wink, "or else your mother might find you in your night clothes."

He watched her blush deepen. She gave him a quick peck on the lips and wiggled down from his arms.

"You'll be wanting to get some clothes on too." She patted his backside and headed for the dresser.

Mo chuckled. Life with Lizzy was already bringing more joy and excitement into his life than he'd had since he moved to Key West eight months ago.

As he had suspected, Cook came in with all four children, saying they'd been up since the crack of dawn wanting to come to their new house. She'd held them off as long as she could. After talking a few moments longer, she left, going on to work at Ellis Southard's home.

The children were all light-hearted. He'd never seen them this talkative before, and before long his head pounded with each syllable they spoke. "Lizzy, I have to run into town for a couple errands. Do ye need anythin'?" He needed a little peace and quiet.

"I could use some fresh fruits and vegetables, and whatever meat you'd like for dinner tonight."

"Done. I'll bring them home with me." He reached for her hand and squeezed it slightly. They'd agreed to limit their physical expressions of affection in front of the children for a while to let them adjust to their mother being married. His first test of holding back and already he wanted to flunk. But Lizzy was counting on him. He wouldn't fail her. He wouldn't fail her children. "Be home as soon as I can." He winked, and his heart overflowed with joy when he saw the sparkle in her eyes.

"Can I come, Mr. Mo?" William asked.

He looked to Lizzy to see if she had any problem with it. Seeing none, he agreed.

"Yipee." William jumped up and down.

"You'll have to behave," Mo cautioned.

William grew somber and promised, "I will." Reaching up,

he took Mo's hand. He had a son, two sons, he realized. *Goodness, life can change mighty fast.* He knew he could never replace the boy's real father, but he could try to be a good example. The problem was that he didn't have a clue.

"Mr. Mo?" William spoke as they walked on the crushed coral path toward town.

"Yes, William?"

"Is Momma going to have a baby?"

❧

"Where'd you hear a fool thing like that?" Lizzy stood stunned at Sarah's question.

"Jimmie Joe says the only reason people get married quickly is 'cause they're going to have a baby."

"Well, Jimmie's wrong." Lizzy wiped her brow. "I'm not having a baby."

"I knew it wasn't so. You won't have a baby, will you, Momma?"

"Oh, Sweetheart, I don't know. That's up to the good Lord and His timing. I'm not planning on having a baby any time soon." Did she even want another child? Still, the idea of having a child born out of her and Daniel's love. . .

"Momma?" Sarah pouted.

"What?"

"You weren't listening to me. I asked if I could give Jimmie Joe a fat lip."

"No. You know I don't cotton to fighting."

Sarah crossed her arms across her chest. "But he said. . ."

"It doesn't matter what he said. It isn't true, and in time the truth will come out. In the meantime, the question is, would Jesus give someone a fat lip because they asked if His momma was having a baby?"

"No."

"Well, then that's your answer to how you should behave." Lizzy began washing the inside of the cupboards. She knew Mo had cleaned the place after James Earl passed on, but apparently cleaning the inside of cupboards wasn't included in his idea of cleaning.

"All right, Momma, but I'd rather give him a fat lip."

"Just see that you don't. That's the real test."

Sarah nodded and headed up the stairs.

A baby! Where'd Jimmie Joe hear a fool thing like that? Probably from his mother. Lizzy sighed. By now all of Key West no doubt believed she and Daniel were expecting. She worried her lower lip. People probably thought they'd been courting for ages, seeing how he came to her house every other night for lessons. "Oh well, ain't much you can do to get a conch back in its shell once it's out."

"What conch?" Ben asked with a mouth full of banana.

"Just rumors."

"Oh, you mean the one about you havin' a baby?" Ben laughed. "Can't believe how silly children can be."

Lizzy eyed her oldest son cautiously. Being all of eight years and a man of the world, she didn't think he even knew how babies were born. She hadn't explained it to him yet.

"And how silly is that?" Did she dare ask?

"Come on, Mom, I'm not a baby. I know where babies come from."

"Well, I suppose you do." What he knew, he hadn't learned from her or her brother, so what exactly he knew could prove interesting. "But why don't you tell me what you've heard?"

Ben rolled his eyes. "You know, you have to kiss under the moonlight. A full moon."

"Ah, I forgot that was a part of it." Lizzy smiled.

"Well, I know you've never kissed Mr. Mo. So I know you're not going to have a baby. Even if you did kiss him yesterday 'cause you got married." Ben wiped his mouth. The very obvious fact that he found kissing girls to be distasteful was something Lizzy found reassuring. "That wasn't a full moon last night."

"Well, kissing has something to do with having a baby, but there's more to it. When you're older I'll have Mr. Mo fill you in on the man's part."

"No thanks. I think Uncle George and Aunt Clarissa kiss all the time, but they're careful about the full moon. So if you start kissing Mr. Mo, watch out for the full moon, Mom."

"Thanks for the warning, Son." Lizzy wasn't going to argue the point, and she certainly didn't want to fill the young man in on the facts of life before he was old enough to understand.

"You're welcome. I like my new room."

"I'm glad."

Lizzy wrung out the rag and wiped the shelves in the cabinet one last time. "There, those are done. Ben, will you chop me some kindling?"

"Sure." He tossed the banana peel over his shoulder and it landed in the trashcan.

No sooner was he out the back door than William came running in through the front door. "Momma, we're home."

A smile rose on her face. The children loved their new home. Or at least loved the adventure of having a new home.

"William, you best go up to your room and settle your things," Lizzy suggested.

"Aw, Ma," William whined.

"Do as yer mother says," Daniel commanded with his deep rich voice and gentle approach.

"Yes, Sir."

Lizzy blinked. "What did you do with the boy while you were in town?"

"We came to an understandin'." Daniel winked.

"Oh, I'm all ears."

"Later, Darlin'. We've got company comin'."

"What?"

"Yer brother and his family are on their way. I saw them when we came up the walkway. We're about three minutes ahead of them."

"Oh."

Daniel walked up beside her and whispered, "There's some rumors."

"Sarah informed me."

Daniel nodded. "I'm sorry, Lizzy. I guess we should have waited a while. I just didn't want ye vulnerable to that—that horrible excuse for a man, Sanchez."

"Hello!" Clarissa called as she pulled the screen door open. "Lizzy, we go away for one day and the whole world changes. What on earth happened?"

Daniel draped his arm across her shoulders. "We got married."

Clarissa rolled her eyes. "No foolin'. So when did you two fall in love?"

seventeen

Daniel and George grilled the fish outside while Clarissa and Lizzy put together some rice, biscuits, and a fresh salad. Daniel's little vegetable garden was a godsend. Unexpected guests for dinner strained the amount of fish he'd brought home, but everyone had a piece, and the rest of the meal was rounded out with the various items the ladies had prepared.

"I thought they'd never leave," Daniel mumbled at the evening's end.

"Me too. I love them and they needed to find out what had happened between us. But I'm glad to be alone now."

"You didn't tell them the full truth?" Daniel whispered, not wanting the children to hear him.

"No, I suppose I didn't. But I don't want everyone to know either."

"I'll not say a word, Lizzy." He stepped up behind her and wrapped his arms around her. He'd been waiting all day for an opportunity to embrace her, to feel her soft skin against his.

Lizzy sighed, and nuzzled into his chest.

"The children seem to like their new home."

"Yes. And it's time for them to be settled in their new beds. Care to lend a hand?"

"Tell me what I need to do," Daniel offered.

"It's easy. Make sure they wash and are dressed for bed. William has to be encouraged to change his undergarments."

Daniel chuckled. "I think that's a male thing. I remember my momma givin' me a tongue lashin' when she found out I hadn't changed mine for a week. I's about William's age at the time."

"I was, not I's."

"Sorry. I'm getting better, but I've been speaking that way

for near thirty years."

"I know, and you're doing wonderfully. Do you mind my correcting you?"

"No, just keep doing it in private. Public, I do mind. But we've been over that before."

"Momma," Sarah whined. "Olivia keeps putting her doll on my pillow."

"It begins," Lizzy whispered into Daniel's ear. He'd released her when Sarah had whined, and now she ached to be back in his arms. How could a person fall so deeply in love in such a short time? Was it love? Or was she just so lonely after not having had a husband around for nearly five years? In either case, Daniel's arms were a place of solace.

After the children were settled, Lizzy sat down at the table with Daniel as he pored over the bookwork Mr. Ellis had given him earlier.

"I just don't understand this. Mr. Ellis has explained it a million times, but it just don't make sense."

"Show me what you know." Lizzy examined the ledger, noting the various columns and figures below each one and beside each name.

"This here is a list of the men who work for Mr. Ellis." He pointed to the column to the left-hand side. "And this here column is where the number of sponges gathered that day is recorded."

Lizzy nodded.

"This is the total of sponges for the week."

He was doing fine so far.

"I just don't understand how he gets the figures in this column."

The payment column for the men, she noted. "How does Mr. Ellis pay the men?"

"By how many sponges he harvests."

"Okay, so how much is that?"

"Some are paid a nickel per sponge, others are paid up to a dime. Depends on how long they been working for him."

"That's recorded in this column, right?"

Daniel nodded.

"So, Toby brought in 125 sponges this week."

Daniel nodded again.

Lizzy continued, "And he gets paid a nickel per sponge."

Daniel knitted his eyebrows and nodded again.

"So he earned six dollars and twenty-five cents."

"How'd ye do that so fast? Yer just like Mr. Ellis. I'm still counting."

"Daniel, do you know how to multiply numbers?"

"What's multiply?"

"It's a way to figure numbers faster than adding every time. First I'll show you a trick for all the men who are earning a dime a sponge. Then I'll explain it for you. If you add a zero after the number of the amount of sponges a man brought in, like Micah's two hundred and thirty here, he earned twenty-three dollars."

"How'd ye do that?" Daniel's eyes rounded with excitement.

"Well, if you have ten bananas and bought another ten how many would you have?"

"Twenty."

"Right, so you could say you had two sets of ten bananas. That's multiplying. Tens and ones are easy. Anything multiplied by one is the same number. Anything multiplied by ten adds a zero. Then we start multiplying by twos, threes. . ." Lizzy went on to explain how to multiply and show Daniel that basically he just had to memorize the multiplication chart, which she proceeded to draw out for him.

"Lizzy, this is amazing. It will save a bundle of time figurin' the men's wages."

She kissed him on the cheek. "Good. Do you mind if we go to bed now? The children will be up early and I've been dragging all day."

Daniel closed the books and got up from the table.

"Thank you, Lizzy. I don't know why Mr. Ellis never told me about multiplying."

"Probably because he didn't realize you've been adding all the time."

"Guess so." Daniel looked down into her eyes. His unspoken request caused her heart to hammer in her chest. She placed her hand into his and followed her husband into their bedroom. Daniel closed the door and locked it shut before he lifted her into his arms. "Oh, Lizzy. . ."

❧

Mo woke feeling on top of the world. He'd gotten up before Lizzy had stirred. He could still feel the pleasure of her full lips on his. They reminded him of sweet plums in both color and taste. Daniel groaned and went to work. He couldn't wait to use the multiplication chart Lizzy had drawn for him last night.

A few men had gathered on the dock. "Mornin', Toby."

"Morning, Mo. How's married life?"

"Wonderful." Mo beamed.

Toby chuckled. "What about having those four young'uns under foot?"

"They's good young'uns, well behaved. Lizzy's done a fine job raisin' 'em."

"Glad you're happy. Me, I like being single." Toby grinned. His dark skin glistened in the sunlight. His yellowing teeth, minus a couple, peeked through his smile.

"Don't think I'll miss being single." Mo reached over and grabbed some nets with his good hand. "Better get out there, time's a wastin'," he encouraged Toby.

"Whatever. I bring in my share."

Daniel remembered that Toby's share was typically far less than that of most of the other men. And he could see why Mr. Ellis kept him at the lower pay rate. Often there were days when Toby didn't even bother to come to work. "Ye might try doin' a little more spongin' than sleepin' in yer boat."

Toby looked over at Daniel and narrowed his gaze. "What?"

"I've seen yer skiff just floatin' and ye layin' in it more

than once. You'd earn more if ye worked more."

"I earn enough."

Daniel couldn't imagine how. Of course, Toby had the kind of life he'd never been inclined toward. "Yer choice." He glanced past Toby. "Mornin', Mr. Ellis." Mo watched Toby lighten a shade of brown.

"Morning, Mr. Ellis," Toby coughed out.

"Morning, Toby." Ellis stepped up to Mo. "I didn't expect you to make it this morning."

"I'm feeling fine. Need to keep the hand clean, but I'm in good shape otherwise."

"Just the same, after you get the men off, you can go home with the books. I don't need them done until tomorrow."

"Lizzy showed me how to multiply last night."

"You didn't know? I'm sorry, I just assumed. . ." Ellis's words trailed off.

"It's all right. She showed me. And I think I can get the hang of it now. She wrote me a multiplication chart but says I have to memorize it."

Ellis chuckled. "She is a good teacher."

Mo laughed. "Yes, Sir, she is."

❧

Day after day, week after week, Mo found himself coming to work with more joy than he'd known in a lifetime. How could one woman change a man's life so much? They'd been married a month now. The stitches were out and he was back to work full time. Every evening he'd come home to a clean house, a table full of food, and an increasing wonder at just how amazing God was to have given him such a gift.

They talked and talked every evening. He was surprised to find he had stuff to talk about. He'd always been a quiet man, didn't give much time to chewing the fat with others; with Lizzy, though, he couldn't stop himself. He found he wanted to share his day, and she wanted to know. "Amazin', Lord."

Mo dove into the crystal waters once again. His skiff was fully loaded, but he wanted to fill the net one more time. He pulled and cut the sponges and moved on to the next one, leaving the smaller ones to continue to grow for harvesting another day.

Breaking the surface for air, he sucked in a deep breath and went down again. Tropical fish swam up beside him. He delighted in their vivid blues and reds, so unlike the black and brown catfish he'd catch from the river up North. Catfish did make some good eating, even though they were such an ugly fish.

Ye know, Lord, I'm still amazed that Lizzy finds me desirable. I'm not a handsome man. And the scars. . .well, they don't improve my image none.

Mo kicked back to the surface. He had a good haul for the day. The sun was getting halfway between the high point and the horizon. He'd have enough time to go over the books again. He'd memorized the multiplication chart, and that was a blessing.

Once back in the boat, the wind shifted direction. Mo looked up to the sky and then froze. A funnel cloud was forming to his left.

❧

Lizzy beat the rug again and more dust formed a cloud around her. The house was shaping up nicely. She'd even had enough time to do some planting in Daniel's garden. The kids seemed to enjoy their new home, but they did miss their cousins. Today she'd let them go to George's for the afternoon and dinner. Tonight she planned an intimate dinner for two.

Lizzy wagged her head. She and Daniel had been married for a month, and she found herself falling more and more in love with him. And yet she was more and more afraid to admit it. Telling Daniel she loved him seemed somehow to lessen her love for Ben. She knew in her head Ben would be pleased that she'd found someone to spend her days with, that he'd be happy for her and the children. But the reality was she was beginning to feel more and more disloyal to her original marriage vows. She'd pray every day, reminding erself that their vows were meant to last only until death. ut she couldn't release herself from those vows.

Lizzy reached out and whacked the rug yet again. Working n the rug helped work through her confused emotions.

"Trying to kill it?" Bea called out.

"More like using it for target practice," Lizzy quipped.

"Uh-oh. What's wrong? Which one of your little ones is in ouble now?"

"No one. Nothing's wrong."

"Come on, something's bothering you. Spill it."

Lizzy smiled. Bea coming by was an answer to prayer. She eeded someone to talk with, and her mother wasn't the one ight now. "I'm feeling disloyal to Ben because I'm falling in ove with Daniel."

"Oh." Bea stepped up beside her. "Come on in the house nd pour us some limeade. I need to get off my feet for a pell."

"I could use the break." Lizzy leaned the broom up against he hanging rug and led Bea into the house.

Lizzy went to the sink and pumped out some fresh water o rinse herself off before serving up the refreshing drink.

"So, how bad is the ghost of Ben?" Bea asked, easing her wollen body into a chair.

"Not too bad, but I almost called Daniel 'Ben' at a very inppropriate time," Lizzy confessed.

"Oh dear. That wouldn't encourage a new husband to hear is wife calling out her previous husband's name."

"No, and Daniel's so vulnerable. I can't make that mistake. Ie's such a tenderhearted man."

"You really do love him, don't you?"

"I suppose I do. I just can't tell him. I wouldn't want him o feel I was pressuring him into loving me."

"Excuse me? You're married."

"Yes, but. . ."

"But you didn't marry him for love?"

"Right."

"Do you think he doesn't love you?"

"I honestly don't know. There are moments when he looks at me and I get so weak in the knees. I'd swear he believes I'm the best thing in his life. But then there are moments when we don't connect. He's had such a different life, such a hard life. So many people have hurt him in the past. And not all of them used a whip. I can't hurt him. I just can't."

"You think by telling Daniel you have these thoughts of Ben he'll be hurt?"

"Yes. I can't apologize for my life with Ben. I loved Ben with all the passion two people can enjoy. But with Daniel it's different."

"Because?"

"Well for one thing, I didn't fall in love with him the first moment I saw him. In fact, I was frightened by him. He's so big."

Bea giggled. "He is a giant. But you got past that."

"Of course, or I'd never have started teaching him."

"Hmm, are you still teaching him?"

"Yes."

"Is it necessary?" Bea took a sip of her drink.

"He has so much to learn. He's doing wonderfully but. . ."

Bea cut her off. "Lizzy, he's your husband. Did you teach Ben?"

"No, he could read. At least, I thought he could read." Lizzy rubbed the back of her neck. "You know, I never got one letter from Ben once he went off to war. I figured it was a problem with the mail. But he never read to the children. He'd sit and listen and encourage them in their lessons, but he. . . Do you suppose Ben just hid it from me?"

"It's possible. I've seen many folk who pretended to know how to read when in fact they couldn't."

"But. . .why should I stop teaching Daniel? He's so anxious to learn."

"I'm not saying you shouldn't answer questions he might have. I'm just saying that a man needs to feel he's the head of the household, and with you being in command of the teaching, well, he might not feel that way. On the other hand, you also may not see him as head, like Ben was."

"I wouldn't. . .I don't think. . .I mean. . . Oh goodness. Do you think that's the problem? By not giving Daniel his rightful place as head of the household I keep putting Ben back in it?"

"Might be some of it. The other fact is simpler—Ben was your husband. You loved him. War took him away from you. Daniel will understand that. I think you should talk with him about it."

"I can't, Bea. He'll be so hurt. He'll feel like I don't love him."

"He probably already feels that. You said you can't tell him you love him. Which means you haven't said it, right?"

Lizzy hung her head. "No, I haven't told him I love him."

"Why not?"

"I don't know. I suppose because I feel I'm being disloyal to Ben. But I guess that really isn't the whole problem. I don't know if he loves me. I'm afraid to be vulnerable, to open my heart and have the man not respond the same way."

"That's the real problem. You don't trust Mo."

"I do. He's wonderful to me and the children."

"Nope, sorry. You don't. If you did you'd open your heart and tell him how you feel."

eighteen

Mo rowed in as fast as he could. Funnel clouds on the ocean weren't that unusual, but gray ones were. By the time he reached the dock, he found Ellis already battening down the hatches, netting the sponges and tying them down to the pilings—anything to save them from the fierce wind that appeared to be coming fast.

"Good haul, Mo."

"Thanks. I think I beached it high enough off the shore line."

Ellis glanced at the shore. "Should be safe."

"I covered the skiff with the netting. Shouldn't lose the sponges unless we lose the skiff." Mo grabbed some nets and climbed up on top of the shed to gather the sponges there. "Do ye want me to slack the lines on your boat, Mr. Ellis?"

"If you get to it before me, sure."

Slack lines would give the boat the ability to ride the waves without being pulled back by the dock it was anchored to. Mo finished gathering the sponges on the roof and hustled down the ladder. "What should I tie these to?"

"Anything. After the storm they'll need to be cleaned and dried again. I just don't want to lose them."

Mo nodded and tied the netted sponges between two pilings, fishing a rope through the opened ends of the net so the sponges wouldn't be blown out of his hammock-like storage spot. Pulling in Ellis Southard's personal sailboat, he jumped on board and moved it between the dock and a couple of posts that stood loosely in the harbor. The lines set, he pulled the boat back toward the dock. Mo spanned the three-foot gap, thankful he had long legs. The outer poles would keep the boat from hitting the dock. The ties to the dock would keep the boat from hitting the outer poles, and all four should keep it from being torn out to sea or dumped up on shore. In the end it would depend on the size of the storm.

"Mo!" Ellis hollered. "I can't get these ropes free."

"If ye can't, the storm probably can't either," Mo quipped as he went to help Ellis.

Ellis Southard was a relatively strong man, but there had been more than one occasion where Mo's strength had come in mighty handy. Day by day he was feeling more useful, a needed part of a community, something he'd never felt before in his life.

The two men continued to work. Other men brought in their skiffs loaded with sponges. They pulled each boat up on shore and turned them over, leaving the sponges inside the skiffs.

"Do ye think it's a hurricane?" Mo asked as they looked at the darkening horizon.

"Not likely—too early in the season. Probably just a good storm."

"Ifin ye don't need me any longer, I'd like to get home and take care of the house."

"We're set here. Go home, Mo. And thanks." The other men had left as soon as they had their skiffs up on shore. No one bothered to count each man's haul. And Mo figured some of the men might claim to have brought in more than they actually had, but there wasn't much he could do about that.

"See ye tomorrow." Mo headed toward shore.

"If the storm passes—if not stay home with your new bride." Ellis grinned.

Mo found himself grinning as well at the prospect. Life with Lizzy had become so special.

His smile slipped. The love he felt for her was so deep and so real it scared him. He wanted to tell her how he felt; he longed to tell her. But they hadn't gotten married because of love. A mutual respect for one another, yes—but not love.

Could he risk his fragile marriage with a declaration of love? Mo quickened his pace toward home.

The wind whipped at his shirt. The air held an unusual warmth, and its smell was peculiar. He'd never seen a storm quite like this before. He broke into a run. He'd have to hurry to get the house's windows boarded up. Thankfully, he'd fixed the shutters last week. The cistern was clean, and the drainage tubes from the roof he'd cleaned last month. He'd plug the opening to the cistern for the first few minutes of rain. Then he'd open it so clean, fresh water would fill it. He'd hoped to enlarge the cistern with Lizzy and the children living with him, but he hadn't gotten up the extra funds for such a large project. For James Earl the small cistern would have served him quite well. For a family of six, it wouldn't be enough during the dry season. Luckily, they were just beginning the rainy season. He had time to build a larger cistern.

Mo found Lizzy outside, closing the shutters over the windows. "Where's the children?"

"They went to my brother's for the afternoon and dinner. I think they may end up spending the night, from the looks of this storm."

"I hope so. I wouldn't want to see them out in this. Do ye need me to go runnin' over there and tell them to stay put?"

"No, I need you to help me. I'm afraid I didn't see this storm coming until a few moments ago."

Mo reached up beside his wife and clasped the shutter she was struggling with. "Go inside. I'll take care of these."

"I'm glad you're home."

Her eyes were red from tears. He reached out and cupped her face. "Lizzy?"

"Not now, Daniel. Later, after we've got the house ready for the storm."

"All right." His heart twisted in his chest. Something had hurt her. Could it be those silly rumors about her expecting? Somehow he didn't suspect that was the case. Lizzy didn't appear to be the kind of woman who would be hurt by idle chatter. No, something else was wrong. The question was if he was man enough to handle it.

He hit the wall of the house with his fist. "God, give me strength. I don't know what I'll do if Lizzy tells me our marriage is a mistake."

❧

Lizzy washed her face one more time. Why was she still crying? Bea left hours ago. The reality was she was afraid. Afraid of the truth. Afraid to completely trust her husband. Bea had nailed the problem on the head. She needed to confess her fears and concerns about Ben, about her near slips at calling Daniel by Ben's name. If she wanted God to be the center of their marriage, she needed to be honest and open with Daniel.

But was he ready for that kind of a relationship? He kept so many things to himself. Oh sure, they talked most evenings. But so many times he avoided the deep secrets of his past, which in turn had her keeping her memories of Ben and their marriage to herself as well. He hadn't said another word about Caron, what she was like, how hurt he was. Could they really build a marriage on so many hidden secrets, hidden hurts? Could they ever open up completely and become that threefold cord the Bible spoke about?

Perhaps in time. She shouldn't push it. Not now. The marriage was too fragile.

Lizzy finished arranging the table for their dinner. The romantic dinner she'd planned would be lost to the storm and her worries about their marriage. How could she hide this from Daniel? He'd already seen she'd been crying.

She wrung the linen napkin in her hands. The longing to tell Daniel her feelings was so strong she wondered if the good Lord was trying to squeeze it out of her.

The front door opened and closed with a bang. "Sorry," Daniel offered, as he headed down the hall toward her. He leaned down and gave her a quick peck on the lips. "I need to wash up." He glanced at the table. "What's this?"

"A romantic dinner for two." She winked.

"Then why the tears?" He stumbled over to the sink and pulled off his shirt.

Lizzy walked up to him and traced the lines on his back. "These," she mumbled. She felt his muscles stiffen under her fingertips.

"What about 'em?" He continued to pump the water into the sink.

"Daniel, I need to talk about your past. I need to talk about my past. I know you married me for my protection, but I believe God doesn't want us to have a marriage in name only. He wants to draw us close to each other. I. . .I. . ." She fought the fiery blaze of salty tears filling her eyes. "I just think we need to talk."

"Haven't we been doing that? I told ye where those scars came from," he huffed.

"Forget it, you're right. I shouldn't have brought it up." She pulled her hand away from his back. He stomped into their room and closed the door.

Why, oh why, had she listened to Bea? She should have kept her mouth shut, should have kept to her resolve that now wasn't the time or the place, that their marriage was too young for this kind of deep conversation.

Lizzy could hold back the tears no longer. The walls of the kitchen seemed to be closing in on her, and she pushed herself out the door into the back yard. "Why didn't I keep my mouth shut, Lord? I knew he wasn't ready to open up." She fought the wind and walked around the back yard. Her skirt whipped past her, creating a sail. The dark gray sky sizzled with lightning.

❧

Mo kicked the chair. Why had he spoken so harshly to Lizzy? She only wanted to get closer. Didn't he want that? Didn't he hope and pray she would come to love him in the same way he'd come to love her? "So why am I pushing her away, Lord?"

Mo fumbled with the buttons on a fresh, clean shirt. *A*

romantic dinner—she planned a romantic dinner, and instead we're having our first fight. You messed up big time, old boy. He stared at the dark reflection of himself. The years had taken their toll. He wasn't the same handsome lad of his youth. His body was scarred; his heart was scarred—and yet Lizzy had still married him. She even honored the commitment of intimacy between a husband and wife. How could she possibly. . . Mo rubbed his hands over his face. Echoes of Caron's flattering words pulled him back to his past.

"Danny, you're so handsome, all the girls envy me."

He caressed her cheek.

"Mother says we can marry next month."

"I's happy about that."

"The master, he wants to see me tomorrow. Do you think he'll make me a house slave?"

Daniel didn't think that was his intention at all. He'd watched the master watching him and Caron for weeks now. No, his intent for Caron was far worse. "Don't go, Caron."

"You know I can't disobey the master." Caron sat in his lap.

He wanted to make her his wife right then and there, but a Christian man was to wait and honor the Lord. "Please, Caron, don't go."

"Don't be silly, the master probably heard about our wedding and wants to congratulate us."

"Ifin that's so, then how's come he didn't ask to see me too."

Caron shrugged her shoulders.

"Please, Caron. Don't go."

"You know I can't disobey the master. I ain't 'bout to be whipped like you."

And that was the truth of it. Caron was a good slave, always doing what was expected of her. She never complained, not even once. He, on the other hand. . . Well, he had a mind of his own sometimes, and that just seemed to get him in more and more trouble.

Mo blinked and came back to the present, to the man in the mirror, no longer a slave, no longer bound to a woman who found. . . No, he wouldn't think about that again. It was over, done with.

"Lizzy?" he called. Hearing no answer, he opened the door.

"Lizzy?" he called again.

No answer.

He stepped into the kitchen. She wasn't there. The room was dark. The storm was upon them. His palms started to sweat. Sulfur filled his nostrils as he lit the candle on the table and the oil lamp on the wall.

"Lizzy, where are ye?"

The back door banged in its casing. He caught a glimpse of her in the back yard, bent over, holding her sides. Mo's heart twisted in his chest. He'd hurt her. He hurt her bad.

Mo ran to the door and stepped out. "Lizzy!" he hollered against the wind. Bits of sand and coral stung his face and chest. He needed to get her inside. Mo stepped closer, holding onto the railing. The wind sucked his breath away.

"Lizzy!" He leapt from the stairs, sprinting across the yard. He pulled her up from the ground. Tears streamed down her face. "Oh, Baby, I'm sorry." He held her as tightly to his chest as he could without breaking her ribs. How could he have been such a fool? How could he have hurt someone so precious to him? How could he. . . ?

Lizzy collapsed in his arms. "Lizzy!"

nineteen

"Lizzy darling, please wake up." Mo laid her on their bed. He had examined her for cuts and bruises and found none. *Why has she fainted, Lord? Please, show me what to do.*

She groaned.

"Lizzy, wake up, Girl." Mo brushed her lips with his own. "I'm sorry, Honey, I didn't mean to get so upset." Her eyelids flickered open and closed. "Come on, Darlin'. Come back to me."

She opened her hazel eyes, her pupils dilated and unfocused. "That's it, Honey, wake up."

"What?" A hoarse whisper escaped her throat.

"Ye fainted in my arms, Honey." He pushed a few strands of wayward hair from her mocha cheeks. "Are ye feelin' sick?"

"I haven't eaten much today."

"Can I get ye somethin'?" He eased off their bed.

"No, stay, Daniel. We need to talk."

"All right. I'm sorry about earlier. You're right, I've kept some of the darkest parts of my past hidden from ye. I don't want your head soiled with such horrible memories."

"And I've hidden things from you," she confessed.

"Ben?"

A gentle, rosy blush painted across her cheeks. "Yes. I loved him, Daniel. I–I. . ."

"Of course ye loved him. That doesn't bother me."

"Really?"

"Of course not. You married him for love. I could never take that place in your heart."

"That's the problem, Daniel, you are."

"What are ye sayin'?" He laid down beside her and cradled her in his arms.

"I've fallen in love with you, Daniel Greene. I know you didn't marry me for love, and I don't expect you to love me the way I love you. . ."

"Hold it right there, Woman. Ye love me?"

Tears filled her eyes. "Yes, I'm sorry."

"Silly woman. Don't ye be sorry for loving me. I just can't believe ye can. I'm not worthy of your love."

Lizzy propped herself up on one elbow. "Daniel, I don't ever want to hear you say that. You are the most tender-hearted man I know. You've won my heart, pure and simple. God's blessed me by giving me a man like you as my husband. Don't ever put yourself down again."

She loves me, Lord. His heart raced with joy—and fear.

"Honey," she continued, "your body may have scars, and I suspect your heart has some too, but they are nothing compared to the beautiful man you are. You're a wonderful husband, a good provider. Ben had trouble providing for his family. He had a bit too much of the wandering spirit in him. Don't get me wrong, he was a good man, but he'd start thinking about things, and before I knew it, he'd be out there plotting and planning. When news of the war came I knew he'd go. It fit in with his desire to free the slaves. He'd read *My Bondage, My Freedom*, or rather, he'd listened while I read. . ."

"Ben didn't know how to read?"

"Well, I always thought he did, but since I've been working with you, and since there's been some time since I've been with Ben, I'm starting to see that he may not have known how to read. Or if he did, it wasn't very well. He always said, 'I love to hear you read; it's like the gentle call of an evening bird song'—or some other romantic thing. To make a long answer short, no, I don't think he knew how."

"For some reason, I always figured Ben was the perfect husband and an educated man."

"He was smart, don't get me wrong. But he was far from the perfect husband. Personally, I don't think there is a perfect husband, just a husband that's perfect for a particular wife."

"Do ye think I'm perfect for ye?" Mo leaned over and kissed the nape of her neck.

Lizzy groaned. "Yes."

"Great, because I love ye and I can't believe God's blessed me so much with such a wonderful gift as ye."

"You love me?"

"With all my heart, Lizzy. I have for a very long time. I've just been afraid to tell ye."

"Me too."

"There's something else you're keepin' from me."

"What?"

"Ye haven't been eating right lately."

"No, I've been so worked up about Ben and feeling I've been betraying my wedding vows, my stomach's just been a bundle of nerves."

Mo traced his finger down her side and placed his hand lovingly on her stomach. "Oh, I thought maybe. . ."

Lizzy's eyes opened wide. "Do you want a child?"

"Ifin the good Lord gives us one, I'd be happy, yes. But with ye having four already, I'd understand if ye don't want another."

Lizzy rolled to her side and snuggled up to Daniel. "I've just been so emotional lately. I almost called you 'Ben' when, when. . .well, you know. And it shocked me."

Daniel chuckled. "Ye have called me 'Ben,' Darlin', and never knew it. I wasn't offended. I felt somehow connected to ye on a deeper level. Does that make sense?"

"I did?"

"Yes."

"I didn't mean to. I'm sorry."

"Forgiven. Tell me about Ben, how you fell in love."

"Do you really want to know this?"

"Yes. He's a part of ye, Lizzy. That will never change. Your relationship with Ben helped mold ye into the woman I fell in love with. Now I might be jealous that he's the one that gave ye those four wonderful children, but I'll never be jealous that ye had a good relationship with your husband."

"Well, he didn't look a thing like you."

Mo chuckled and listened to his wife's heart. She told him how she fell in love with Ben the first moment she'd laid eyes on him, how they had a whirlwind courtship and married as soon as her mother and father had allowed it. She explained how Ben had two passions in his life and how she shared the same passions. One was her and the children, the other was justice for Negroes. And while they talked the wind howled and whistled through the shutters.

❧

Lizzy couldn't get over the fact that Daniel loved her. Of course, he had treated her as someone special all along, but he'd never proclaimed his love before. But today, lying on their bed together, he'd confessed his love half a dozen times.

"I love ye, Honey, but I'm starvin'. Do we have anythin' to eat?"

"Oh no." Lizzy jumped from the bed. "I had a special dinner warming in the oven."

"Let's hope the fires burned down before the food burned up."

Lizzy ran to the oven and opened the door. A charred layer crusted the pastry she had laid over the meat pie.

"Hmm, a little on the done side," Daniel teased.

"Slightly. We can take off the top layer of pastry and see if the insides are fine."

"You're a wonderful cook, Lizzy. I'm sure if this isn't okay we can find something else."

She nodded and took a fork and lifted the black crust off the meat pie. Sniffing the pie, she smiled. "I think it's okay."

"I'll get some crackers from the cupboard to take the place of the crust."

Crackers sounded wonderful. Her nerves had worked havoc on her system. Even after not eating all day, she had little desire to fill her stomach. Just one sniff of the pie and she felt her stomach roll.

"Lizzy?"

"Hmm?"

"Are ye sure you're all right?"

"My stomach isn't feeling too good. I really got myself worked up over nothing. I'm sorry."

"Think nothin' of it, Girl. I love ye, ye loves me. Life is great."

Lizzy smiled. Yes, life was good. Now if she could only get her raw emotions to calm down and realize what her brain and heart already knew. She and Daniel would have a good marriage. They would build a good home for themselves and the children.

Lizzy poked at the meat pie, eating a couple chunks of potato and some crackers and water. She didn't dare put anything more in her stomach. Maybe she'd caught a bug.

"Ye don't look well, Lizzy. Are ye sure you're all right?"

"I was just thinking maybe I'm coming down with something."

"A couple of the men haven't come in this week because they weren't well. It's possible you've caught somethin'."

"If you don't mind, I think I'll go to bed." Lizzy pushed the chair from the table.

"I'll clean up. Ye go lie down. I'll be in shortly."

Lizzy felt dizzy again and grasped the table.

"Whoa, come on, Girl. I'll carry you in."

"I can walk," she protested, as she wrapped her arms around his neck.

"Yeah, but this is much nicer." Daniel wiggled his eyebrows, and Lizzy felt the tingles all the way down to her toes. God had really blessed her by giving her this kind and gentle man. *Thank You, Lord,* she praised as she snuggled her head onto Daniel's shoulder.

❧

After a good night's rest, Lizzy welcomed the morning. The storm had passed, and the birds were singing as light filtered its way between the cracks of the shutters. Lizzy watched the dust particles dance in the sunlight. They were so carefree and light, exactly the way she felt this morning after confessing her heart to Daniel. He loved her as much as she loved him; could life be any better?

"Morning, Lover." He reached for her and pulled her back to bed.

Lizzy giggled. "Daniel, you've got to go to work."

Daniel groaned. "Don't remind me. The way that wind howled last night, I'll be cleanin' up that dock for days." He snuggled up beside her. "Besides, the rooster hasn't crowed yet."

"He's probably still in hiding."

"Let's stay in bed and hide too." Daniel tickled her sides.

Lizzy squirmed away.

Daniel sat up in bed. "Glad you're feeling better."

"Nothing a good night's rest didn't cure."

"Good. Can ye cook me up a hearty breakfast before I go to work?"

She fetched her robe. "Sure. Eggs and bacon?"

"To start."

"Daniel Greene, you eat more than the whole lot of us and you haven't got an ounce of fat on you. Where do you put it all?"

They enjoyed their playful banter all through breakfast and then said their morning prayers together.

"Lizzy, I'll open the shutters and then go to work. I don't want ye up on a ladder after ye fainted yesterday."

"I'm fine."

"Maybe so, but I don't want nothin' to happen to ye. I'll take care of the shutters."

"Thank you." It was nice having someone who cared about her who didn't just need her, like the children needed her to look after them constantly.

She wondered how the children had fared through the storm.

Daniel opened the door. "Oh, no."

"What's the matter?"

"We've got someone's battered boat in our front lawn."

"What?" Lizzy ran to the front door. Sure enough, a capsized boat lay dry-docked on their lawn. "Oh my. I didn't realize the storm was so bad." Fear rose in her heart. "Do you think the children are all right?"

"Get dressed. I'll go with ye."

Please God, keep them safe. She knew it was too late for that kind of a prayer, but still she had no idea the storm had been that intense. The bright azure sky didn't show any signs of last night's raging storm.

Daniel wrapped his protective hand around hers. "I'm sure they're all right, Honey. They would have sent someone over if there was a problem."

"I'm sure you're right but. . ."

Daniel squeezed her hand. "I understand."

They walked as fast as her legs would take them. Daniel's gait was much longer than her own. He piled up the distance in one step that would take her two to three. She could tell he was worried about the children despite his reassuring words. *He really loves the children, Lord. Thank You.*

They rounded the corner. Palm trees were down; palm fronds littered the street.

"Late last night I heard what sounded like a train outside our house. I'd say we had a small twister touch down not too far from us."

"God kept us safe."

"Amen to that." He released her hand and put a protective arm across her shoulder. "Ye slept soundly last night."

"My heart relaxed."

His broad smile warmed her. "Mine too. I love ye, Lizzy. I want the children to know I love them too."

"I think they already know."

"I suppose but I wanna tell them. And I wanna tell them how much I love ye."

"Oh, Daniel. Go slow. They'll need time to adjust."

"If ye say so. But I think they already know." Daniel winked.

"Momma." William came running toward them as they neared George and Clarissa's house. "Did you see the storm?"

"Some. Is everyone all right?"

William nodded his head so hard it looked like it could fall off. "The roof came off."

Cold fingers of fear gripped at her spine. "And everyone is fine?"

"Yeah, happened when we were sleeping. It's only part of the roof, Momma."

"Momma." Olivia came running. "Daddy, I missed you."

Daddy? When had Olivia started calling Daniel "Daddy"?

"We missed ye too, Sweetheart." Daniel got down on one knee, and Olivia jumped into his arms.

"Momma, Mr. Mo, we were just getting ready to head over to the house," Ben offered. "We lost the front corner of the roof. Uncle George says he can fix it."

"Let me go give Uncle George a hand." Mo placed Olivia in Lizzy's arms and headed toward the house. Lizzy couldn't help but smile.

"You love him, don't you?" Ben asked.

"Yes, Son. I do."

"Good. He's a good man, Mom. I think Daddy is happy for us."

"I think he is too." She brushed her son's short, nappy hair and pulled him to her side. "I'm so glad you're all safe."

"Uncle George says a twister touched down."

"Daniel thought the same. We have a boat in the front yard."

"I want to see it," Ben clamored.

"You will. Where's Sarah?"

"In the house or out back. She's looking for Kitty."

"Kitty?"

"A kitten. Mrs. Jones's cat had kittens about the time we moved to Mr. Mo's."

In the distance she heard Sarah calling, "Kitty-kitty!"

Lizzy walked toward the house. "How bad is it?"

George stood on the roof with his hands on his hips. "It's repairable."

Daniel stood on the ladder. "I'll lend ye a hand, George. I'll run to town, tell Mr. Ellis, and come on back."

"Thanks. Buildings and I don't get along so well. I can make it so it won't leak, but it won't look pretty."

Daniel chuckled. "I don't knows how purty I'll make it, but it won't look too bad."

"I saw some of your handiwork at your place, Mo. You can come build at mine any time."

A terrible shriek came from the back yard.

twenty

"Sarah?" Lizzy ran to the back of the house. Daniel jumped off the ladder, forgetting to climb down first. Everyone followed the terrible cries of Lizzy's seven-year-old daughter.

George called down from the roof. "She looks just fine from here."

In the middle of the yard, sitting on the ground, Lizzy found Sarah sobbing. Lizzy's heart raced. She tried to control her emotions. *Speak calmly,* she reminded herself. "What's the matter, Sweetheart?"

Slowly Lizzy slid to the ground. Something was in her daughter's lap.

"Kitty's dead." Sarah sniffed.

"Oh, Sweetheart, I'm so sorry."

Daniel sat down beside them. "Are ye sure, Sarah?"

"Kitty's not moving." She wiped her nose with her sleeve.

"Can I see Kitty?" Daniel asked, reaching his hand out ever so slowly.

"Why'd she hafta die, Momma? Why?"

"I don't know, Sweetheart."

"But it's not fair."

How could she deny that? Death was a part of life, but it was a part of the sinful life that we now live on this earth. Death wasn't supposed to happen. And yet it did.

"Sarah," Daniel whispered, "sometimes bad things happen to good people. And sometimes bad things happen to innocent kittens. But God uses these bad things to make us stronger. Look at my wrist, Sarah. What do ye see?"

"Scars." She lifted her gaze to Daniel's. He'd gotten her attention.

Give him the right words, Lord, Lizzy prayed.

"And do ye know how I got these scars?"

Sarah nodded her head, yes. "Because you were a slave?"

"Right. But are thar any shackles on my arms now?"

"No." Sarah knitted her eyebrows.

"That's because God took somethin' bad and turned it around. I'm sorry Kitty is dead. But one day, and it may take quite a few days, you'll only have good memories of Kitty, of all the times ye played with her, petted her."

"Do you still remember the bad things that happened to you as a slave?"

"Yes. But the pain is getting less. Look at what the good Lord has given me, and other people like us. The war is over; the slaves are free. And God's given me a special family that loves me and that I love. My heart hurts because your heart hurts, but I know together we can get over this pain."

Sarah opened her hands. The small animal lay in her skirt. "Mr. Mo, can I call you Daddy?"

"Of course ye can, Sweetheart."

"Momma, is it okay to call Mr. Mo, Daddy?"

"Yes," Lizzy croaked out. Her emotions were running amok again. The salt of her tears burned the edges of her eyelids. God was taking the bad in their lives and making it right again.

"May I take care of Kitty, Sarah?" Daniel asked.

"Yes."

Tenderly Daniel's large dark hands lifted the white and black spotted kitten from Sarah's skirt. It fit completely in the palm of his hand. "Shall we bury her?"

Sarah nodded.

Lizzy went to the storage shed and pulled out a shovel. The children all gathered around Daniel. With very slow and careful movements he wrapped the kitten in his handkerchief and laid it on the ground. Then he took the shovel from Lizzy and proceeded to dig the hole. The solemn assembly watched with calm patience. How could one man engage seven children so much that they didn't move a muscle? *Oh, Lord, he's such a good father. Thank You.*

Lizzy stepped back to the shade of the house. The horror of Sarah's scream and the fact that she'd been so sick the day before had left her weak.

"Are you all right, Lizzy?" Clarissa whispered.

"I'm getting over a bug. I'll be fine."

"Can I get you a cup of tea?"

"Thanks, that would be wonderful."

Clarissa darted into the house. Lizzy sat on the back step and watched Daniel carefully place the wrapped animal into the bottom of the pit he'd just dug. Gently, he placed the first shovel of dirt onto the poor little creature. Sarah sniffled. Soon, each of the children were wiping their eyes. Ben and George Jr. pretended not to shed any tears.

Daniel clasped his hands and bowed his head. All seven children bowed their heads as well.

"Father, God, Ye give life to everythin' that lives. So we give Kitty back to Ye. Help these young'uns to get over the pain. In Jesus' name. Amen."

All seven mumbled, "Amen."

Lizzy found herself saying *amen* as well. But to hear George's "Amen!" from the roof startled her. Not only had Daniel captured the children's and her attention, but he'd also captured George's.

"He's a keeper, Lizzy," George said, staring down at her.

"Yeah, I know."

"Young'uns, I hafta go to work, but I'll be back soon. Will ye help while I'm gone?" Daniel asked.

They all nodded their agreement.

"Lizzy, walk with me part way?"

"Sure."

Clarissa handed Lizzy a cup of iced tea. "Take this with you."

"Thanks."

Daniel escorted her out of the yard and down the street before he began to speak. "I hope I did good with the children."

"You were marvelous."

"Do you mind the children calling me 'Daddy'?"

"No. I'm glad the girls want to call you 'Daddy.' I'm sure the boys will soon."

"I'm honored." Daniel pulled her closer to him. The warmth of his chest deepened the closeness she felt for him. "I can't tell ye how proud it made me feel."

Lizzy stopped and Daniel turned to face her. "I'm especially glad for Olivia. She never knew her father. She never called anyone 'Daddy' before."

"God has blessed me."

"No, Daniel. God has blessed us."

A quirk of a smile slipped up the right side of his face. "I love ye, Lizzy."

"I love you, too."

"I've got to go. Ellis will git a worryin'. I'll git back to your brother's as soon as I'm able."

"I may take the kids home, have them change their clothes, and come back."

"Whatever ye think is best. That roof won't be fixed by the end of the day. I can get it right, but it won't be waterproof tonight. It'll take some materials George doesn't have and, I suspect, will be in short supply if this storm hit many homes."

"You might be right. Should I prepare dinner for everyone at our house? Get the little ones out from under foot?"

"Might be a good idea. Make a large pot of that fish chowder. Have the boys go fishin'. Gotta be some good fishin' right now."

"All right." Lizzy didn't want to release him. She wanted to spend the rest of the day in his arms.

He stepped back.

She leaned into him.

He stepped back again.

She let him slip from her grasp.

"I'll see ye soon, Honey," he whispered, before his lips captured hers.

And then the cool breeze that swept past her lips made her aware that she was still standing in the middle of the road with her eyes closed. She opened them to find Daniel walking toward town. "I'll miss you," she whispered.

He turned and waved. Had he heard her?

❧

"Morning, Mr. Ellis," Mo called from the edge of the street.

"Morning, Mo. It's not too bad, considering."

Mo surveyed the damage. Seaweed lined the shore and lay in heaps on the dock. The netted sponges appeared to be all in their places. "Looks pretty easy to clean up."

"How'd your home survive?"

"Just fine. Someone's boat capsized on my front lawn, though."

Ellis shook his head in wonder. "And you're several blocks from the shore."

"I think it may have been in someone's yard. It didn't appear to have anythin' growin' on the hull."

"You're probably right." Ellis leaned down and pulled the lines to his sailboat.

"How'd she fare?"

"She looks fine. Need to bail her out, though. She's riding low in the water."

"I'll stay and lend ye a hand, but I was wonderin' ifin I could help my brother-in-law. He lost part of his roof last night."

Ellis paused and dropped the line. "Is everyone all right?"

"They're all fine. Kinda scary. The children were there for the afternoon and ended up stayin' the night."

"I'm glad everyone's okay. Can I lend a hand?"

"We're needing to replace the front corner of the roof. I know I can get most of that done with what George has around his house. But new shingles will be in high demand."

"I'll run into town and see what I can find. You go, take care of your family. This can wait until tomorrow. We'll need to wash all the sponges again before we can dry them."

"Thank ye, Mr. Ellis. I appreciate it."

"No problem. Cook would have my hide if I didn't let you go."

Mo chuckled. "I imagine she would. Everythin' all right at your house?"

"Yes. I had a tree lose a good sized branch, but it missed the house. Knocked over a bird feeder I put in last month—but that's nothing."

"Sounds like the good Lord spared us from anythin' major."

"So far. I haven't heard from too many folks, but things are looking pretty good." Ellis headed down the dock with Mo before turning off to town. "I'll see you in a bit, Mo."

Mo headed home and gathered his tools and a couple of two-by-eights he had been saving to help with the roof of the new cistern he planned on building. With the boards over his right shoulder and his toolbox in his left hand, he headed back to George and Clarissa's home.

His joy overflowed when he saw Lizzy and the children heading toward him. "Hi."

"Mr. Mo, can I help you?" Ben asked.

"Honestly, I need ye to help your momma. We've got shutters that need opening and I don't want her goin' up the ladder. She wasn't feeling very good yesterday."

"You're sick, Ma?" Ben asked.

"I'm feeling better, Dear."

"Can I count on ye, Son?" He eyed Ben, man to man, or rather, father to son.

Ben puffed up his chest. "Yes, Sir."

"Thank ye. Your mom might need some other help. There's a boat in our front lawn—no telling how bad the back yard is."

Actually he knew and it wasn't too bad, just debris from downed tree branches and palm fronds. But he didn't want to be looking out for Ben with so little time to do a major repair job on George's roof.

"Can I help Momma?" William asked.

"I'm sure ye can, Son. Your momma is goin' to need all your help."

William beamed.

Mo turned to his wife. "You're looking pale, Lizzy. Are ye okay?"

"I'm fine, just tired."

"Ben, when you're finished helpin' your momma, get George Jr. and catch us a bundle of fish for dinner."

"Yes, Sir."

Lizzy grabbed her stomach.

"Lizzy?"

"I'm fine. Just the thought of cleaning fish made my stomach queasy."

"Can ye clean a fish, Ben?"

"Yeah, not as good as you. But I can do it."

"Okay, ye clean the fish. Sarah, ye help your ma in the kitchen. Liv, ye make sure Momma lies down. And, William, your job will be to clean up the back yard."

All four nodded their heads.

"Lizzy, lie down. I don't want ye gettin' worse."

"I'll try."

He narrowed his gaze, givin' her fair warning he wanted to see that she had lain down. She looked to the ground and slowly raised her gaze. Mo chuckled. "Lizzy, you're a beautiful woman and I love ye, but I need to get to work. Behave for your momma, children."

Olivia waved. "Bye, Daddy."

"Bye, Sweetheart."

Sarah hugged his leg and William hugged the other. *Goodness, Lord, it's hard to leave these people.* It was a good thing he went to work every morning before they woke up. "Love ye all, bye." He stepped forward, the children released him, and he willed himself to go help his brother-in-law, though every last muscle demanded that he turn around and help his family. Yes, *his* family. *Thank Ye, Lord. I'm so blessed.*

❧

Ben worked hard doing his man-sized job. Lizzy was thankful Daniel had taken the time to give each of the children an assignment. As much as she didn't want to admit it, she was starting to feel poorly again. She lay down on her bed, and Sarah stood guard. "Can I get you some water, Momma?"

"No, Sweetheart. I'm fine. I'm just going to rest a bit."

"All right. Olivia and I will do the dishes."

She'd forgotten that they'd just run out of the house this morning without taking care of any of the chores. Lizzy rolled over. She needed to rest. Her eyes flickered shut. Peace swept over her. She went to sleep hearing the girls pump the water.

❧

"You young'uns go clean up now. I'll take care of your momma." Lizzy woke to the distinct sound of her mother's voice. Or had she been dreaming, as often happened when she wasn't feeling well and wanting her mother to come and take care of her? A silly notion, since she was all grown up, but one that would slip in her subconscious once in awhile.

"Mom?"

"Land sakes, Child. What's the matter?" Francine towered over her.

"Just a stomach bug. Has me dizzy and my stomach is uneasy."

"Hmm. What did you have to eat today?"

"A slice of toast and a cup of tea."

"How long have ye been feeling this way, Child?"

"A couple days. Not too long."

"Elizabeth Hunte Greene." Francine placed her hands on her ample hips. "Think, Child, when was your last. . ."

"No, I can't be."

"Well, you've been married a month."

Lizzy's eyes widened. Could she be expecting? She placed her hand on her stomach.

Francine chuckled. "I'm going to be a grandma again."

"It could be a bug."

"And a conch can live outside its shell." Francine wagged her head. "I'll fetch you some crackers and make some tea.

You stay down. I'll take care of the family."

Lizzy groaned. Pregnant? Shouldn't she and Daniel have more time together before they brought a baby into the world? On the other hand, this way there would only be five years difference between the baby and Olivia. *A baby? Diapers.* Lizzy rolled over. *Okay, let's think this through.* When was her last cycle? Two weeks before she got married. Which meant she could be close to four weeks pregnant. How was she going to tell Daniel?

No, Daniel said he'd love to have a child. Apparently she didn't have much say in the matter.

A baby. . . Oh no, Lord, the rumors. People are going to think. . . No, I don't need to worry about what people think. I know, Daniel knows, and You know we weren't in the family way before we were married.

Her mother brought in a cup of tea and a plate of crackers. "Eat what you can, Dear. You need to get something down."

"What am I going to tell Daniel?"

Francine chuckled. "The truth."

"Of course I'll tell him the truth. I meant, how am I going to *tell* Daniel."

"Does he not want children?" Her mother sat down on the bed beside her.

"He does. I'm the one that wasn't sure about having any more. I have four already."

"I know, which surprises me why you didn't figure this out for yourself."

"I just wasn't thinking, I guess."

Francine roared. "Something like that. Tell me, Sweetheart, do you love him?"

"More and more each day, Mom. He's so incredibly gentle and kind."

"He's got a good heart." Francine tapped her gently on her shoulder.

"Yeah."

Francine went to the kitchen. Lizzy heard Ben and George

come in with the fish. Her mother complimented them on the fine job they'd done cleaning them. Lizzy decided to stay in her room a bit longer.

"Momma, are you feeling better?" Olivia asked.

"Some, Sweetheart. Thank you."

"Daddy said to let you sleep."

"Daddy's here?"

"He's out back with Uncle George."

Lizzy leapt out of bed, then realized she shouldn't make quick moves. The smell of fish bubbling in the pot. . .the fast movement. . . She held her stomach.

She fought her body's responses and headed into the kitchen to find her way to the back door. "Daniel, are you finished?"

"Roof's done. Mr. Ellis came by and several of the neighbors and lent a hand. It's shingled and everythin'."

"Wonderful. Are you busy?" Lizzy held the door jam for extra support.

"I'll be in in a second, Honey."

❧

"Smells great, Cook. Where's my wife?" Daniel asked as he kicked off the dirt from his boots on the threshold.

"In your room." Francine gave him a strange smile.

"Lizzy?" Mo stuck his head in the doorway.

"Sit down, Daniel. We need to talk."

"What's the matter? Are ye okay?"

"Oh, I'll be fine."

"Then what's the matter?" Daniel eased down beside her. Her eyes sparkled, but her hands wrung the quilt as if it were her worst enemy's neck.

"I figured out why I'm not feeling well."

"And?" He reached out and placed his hand on top of hers. His heart sank, but no matter what was wrong, they would handle this together.

"I'm going to have a baby."

"A baby!" he boomed.

Lizzy nodded.

"Ya-hoo, Lizzy girl, you've made me the happiest man alive."

"Really?"

"Really." Daniel placed a hand on his wife's flat stomach. "There's a little one growin' inside of ye. I can't be more pleased and more amazed at God's good grace."

A smile lifted Lizzy's deep plum lips. "A few short months ago I prayed for a home, a place of my own for myself and the children. I can't believe God's filled His promise to me from Romans 15:13: 'Now the God of hope fill you with all joy and peace in believing, that ye may abound in hope, through the power of the Holy Ghost.' My hope was a home. Not only did God give me a home, but he gave me a new husband and another child born out of love. I love you, Daniel Greene."

"And I love ye, Lizzy girl. A father. I'm going to be a father! I can't believe it." Daniel threaded his fingers around Lizzy's. "A few months ago I only hoped for a peace from the past, to be able to feel like I was worth somethin'. God has filled us to overflowin'."

❧

Lizzy looked over and saw their bedroom doorway filled with ten faces, all smiling, all staring.

"You're going to have a baby, Momma?" Olivia asked.

"Yes, Sweetheart."

"And I'll be her big sister?" Olivia continued.

"Yes." Lizzy nibbled her lower lip. "But the baby could be a brother."

Ben crossed his arms. "You kissed Mr. Mo, didn't you?"

Lizzy chuckled. "Yes, Son."

"Under the moon." Ben shook his head. "I told ya that's how you get babies," he lectured.

The house erupted in laughter. God had filled their house with joy. The past would leave its mark, like the scars on Daniel's wrists and back, but the heart could still find the peace, the hope, and the joy of the Lord.

A Letter To Our Readers

Dear Reader:

In order that we might better contribute to your reading enjoyment, we would appreciate your taking a few minutes to respond to the following questions. We welcome your comments and read each form and letter we receive. When completed, please return to the following:

Rebecca Germany, Fiction Editor
Heartsong Presents
PO Box 719
Uhrichsville, Ohio 44683

1. Did you enjoy reading *Lizzy's Hope* by Lynn A. Coleman?
   - ❑ Very much! I would like to see more books by this author!
   - ❑ Moderately. I would have enjoyed it more if ______________________________

     ____

     ____

2. Are you a member of **Heartsong Presents**? Yes ❑ No ❑
   If no, where did you purchase this book? ______________________________

   ____

3. How would you rate, on a scale from 1 (poor) to 5 (superior), the cover design? ______________________________

4. On a scale from 1 (poor) to 10 (superior), please rate the following elements.

   _____ Heroine _____ Plot

   _____ Hero _____ Inspirational theme

   _____ Setting _____ Secondary characters

5. These characters were special because______________

____

____

6. How has this book inspired your life?______________

____

____

7. What settings would you like to see covered in future **Heartsong Presents** books?______________

____

____

8. What are some inspirational themes you would like to see treated in future books?______________

____

____

9. Would you be interested in reading other **Heartsong Presents** titles? Yes ❑ No ❑

10. Please check your age range:

❑ Under 18 ❑ 18-24 ❑ 25-34

❑ 35-45 ❑ 46-55 ❑ Over 55

Name ______________________________

Occupation ______________________________

Address ______________________________

City ______________ State ______________ Zip ______________

Email ______________________________

NEW MEXICO *Sunrise*

Join the Lucas, Monroe, and Dawson families as they stake their claim to the "Land of Enchantment." Their struggles and triumphs blend into the sandstone mesas and sweeping sage plains of New Mexico, and their tracks are still visible along the deeply rutted Santa Fe Trail and the chiseled railways they traveled. Award-winning author Tracie Peterson brings their stories to life.

NEW MEXICO *Sunset*

The saga of the Lucas, Monroe, and Dawson families, introduced in *New Mexico Sunrise,* echoes across the vast open landscape of a state in its infancy. Now the next generation must take up the pioneer spirit of their parents and lay claim to their place in a changing world.

paperback, 464 pages, 5 3/16" x 8"

♥ ♥ ♥ ♥ ♥ ♥ ♥ ♥ ♥ ♥ ♥ ♥ ♥ ♥ ♥ ♥ ♥ ♥

Please send me ____ copies of *New Mexico Sunrise* and ____ copies of *New Mexico Sunset*. I am enclosing $5.97 for each. (Please add $2.00 to cover postage and handling per order. OH add 6% tax.)

Send check or money order, no cash or C.O.D.s please.

Name____

Address______________________________________

City, State, Zip________________________________

To place a credit card order, call 1-800-847-8270.

Send to: Heartsong Presents Reader Service, PO Box 721, Uhrichsville, OH 44683

♥ ♥ ♥ ♥ ♥ ♥ ♥ ♥ ♥ ♥ ♥ ♥ ♥ ♥ ♥ ♥ ♥ ♥